The Hardy Boys®
in
The Clue of the Screeching Owl

P9-BID-118

This Armada book belongs to:

Mark Voran

The Hardy Boys® Mystery Stories

The Clue of the Screeching Owl

Franklin W. Dixon

Armada

First published in the U.K. in 1972 by
William Collins Sons & Co. Ltd., London and Glasgow.
First published in Armada in 1974 by
Fontana Paperbacks,
8 Grafton Street, London W1X 3LA.

This impression 1983.

Printed in Great Britain by
William Collins Sons & Co. Ltd., Glasgow.

THE HARDY BOYS is a trademark of
Stratemeyer Syndicate, registered in the
United States Patent and Trademark Office.

CONTENTS

*At that moment two venomous snakes slithered
out of the cave*

-1-

Puma Charge!

"SUMMER holidays!" Chet Morton exclaimed. "No more school until September."

The stout, good-natured boy lounged half asleep between Frank and Joe Hardy in the front seat of a powerful yellow convertible. With a soft purr, the car moved swiftly past the carefully tilled fields of the Pennsylvania Dutch farmers.

Dark-haired, eighteen-year-old Frank Hardy was at the wheel. He kept his eyes upon the road which would lead them to the green bulk of the Pocono Mountains later that sunny June afternoon.

Meanwhile, his blond-haired younger brother Joe said, "There used to be witches round here, Chet. See that sign? It's to ward them off."

He pointed to a brightly painted circular design on a huge red barn.

Chet Morton had opened an eye as the car moved past the barn. "What is it?" he asked.

"A hex sign," Joe told him. "Supposed to keep off lightning and protect the farm against witches."

"Witches!" The plump boy straightened up, looking worried. "Today?"

"Sure," Joe Hardy went on teasingly. "If a witch puts a spell on your cow, she won't give milk. Those circles keep off the curse."

9

Nervously Chet looked at the next two barns, at the blue sky above him, and then once all around him.

"Aw, nobody believes in that kind of stuff any more. This is the twentieth century. Stop kidding me, will you, fellows? This is a holiday. All I'm going to do is sleep and eat. Let's not have any mysteries!"

While their friend settled down and closed his eyes once more, Frank and Joe exchanged knowing grins. As sons of the internationally famous detective, Fenton Hardy, they had many times been drawn into baffling and dangerous mysteries, where their brilliant sleuthing had earned them fine reputations of their own. Easygoing Chet Morton, the Hardy's best friend, always seemed to become involved.

"Well, Chet," Frank said, "you may as well know the truth. This isn't just a camping trip. We have to look up Dad's old friend, Captain Thomas Maguire. He's living in a cabin at the edge of Black Hollow, somewhere in those mountains just ahead of us."

"*Captain* Maguire?" repeated the stout boy suspiciously. "What kind of captain is he?"

"A police captain—that is, he was chief of police until five or six years ago. He's retired now."

"I knew it!" Chet exploded. "I just knew it! Another mystery! A fellow no sooner gets set to enjoy a nice, quiet holiday than the Hardys drag him into some detective work.

"When the police and the Hardys get together, it spells trouble. Trouble for old Chet especially. All right—I may as well hear the worst. What is it this time?"

"Well," Frank answered, "there have been some funny goings-on round Black Hollow. Captain Maguire wrote to Dad. He didn't give any details, but asked him to come up and investigate."

"Unfortunately, Dad couldn't make it," Joe took up the story. "He's been working with the New Jersey State Police—not very far from here, in fact—on a new hijacking racket. Among other things, somebody has been stealing shipments of instruments that go into the nose cones of guided missiles. They're taken while being trucked to the assembly station."

"That's important, all right," Chet agreed.

"Dad heard about our camping trip and suggested we take it near Captain Maguire's cabin," Frank finished.

"Well, Chet—shall we turn back?" Joe needled. He and Frank knew that underneath his complaints, their friend had plenty of courage—and even more curiosity.

"I suppose we can't call it off now," Chet mumbled. "All our food would go to waste!"

It was mid-afternoon when the prosperous valley of the Pennsylvania Dutch, lush with the tender green of young crops, had been left behind. The road climbed and curved up a heavily wooded hill. Now and then the thick foliage on either side was broken by a smooth grey rock face.

"We're really in the mountains," Joe noted.

After topping a ridge, the road descended and then straightened out as it approached the next line of hills. Frank, looking ahead, could see the buildings of a town.

Suddenly the stillness was broken by the raucous sound of music and voices blaring over a loud-speaker. They strained their eyes to see where it came from.

"I see it!" Chet shouted.

A number of tents came into view. A bright, gay banner on top of one read:

KLATCH'S CARNIVAL

"Whoops!" Chet shouted eagerly. "Let's go in, fellows. I can smell the popcorn from here!"

Laughing, Frank parked the convertible, and the three boys entered the carnival. Now the d.n of the loud-speakers was overwhelming. Crowds of people moved in both directions. The rides—the "Whip", the "Octopus", and several others whirled madly. The people on them screamed shrilly. Stall keepers were shouting from side-show platforms.

Chet immediately bought himself a carton of popcorn, a bag of peanuts, and a frothy cloud of pink candyfloss.

"Say, how about this?" Joe asked. He pointed to a sign:

COLONEL BILL THUNDER
Fearless Animal Trainer

The roar of some wild animal, coming from within the tent, was enough to convince the boys of the colonel's courage. In a moment Frank, Joe, and Chet had entered and taken seats.

In the centre of a large circular cage stood a man dressed in a white shirt, white riding breeches, and shining black boots. His thick, dark hair, moustache, heavy eyebrows, piercing eyes, and the black whip that he held coiled in one hand gave him a look of authority. He needed it, for seated on small stools at equal distances round the cage were four huge cats.

Two were tawny, two black. All four glared at the man, their long tails flicking nervously.

"Pumas," Joe whispered to his companions. "Big ones, too."

The black whip snapped. The trainer's body rotated as he forced each powerful animal, in turn, to leave its stool and then mount it again.

"This fellow's really good," Frank declared. "Notice how his back is fully exposed to one of the cats at all times."

But even as Frank spoke, the snarling black animal upon which the trainer had just turned his back gathered itself and sprang!

"He'll be killed!" shrieked Chet, dropping popcorn, peanuts and candyfloss to the ground.

Warned by the boy's shout, Colonel Thunder whirled to face the charging beast. With a series of lightning-like whip snaps he drove the snarling cat back to its place.

"Terrific!" declared Chet to a man beside him.

"He's good all right," the stranger agreed. "Had another cat that almost got him, though—big yellow devil. Had to get rid of him finally."

Spellbound, the boys watched the rest of Colonel Thunder's act, and then continued their journey.

At the end of the afternoon, two hours later, the yellow convertible, climbed slowly up a steep dirt road with high, dark woods on either side.

"I think we're going in the right direction," Frank said. "But we'd better check. There's a house."

The bright-yellow car came to a stop before a weather-beaten timber building with a paling fence in front. The place was silent.

"Seems deserted," Joe commented, looking around.

As the three approached the gate, however, Frank suddenly pointed to a path amongst the trees at the side of the house.

"Here's somebody!"

A thin, worried-looking woman emerged from the woods dragging a boy about seven years old by the hand. He was crying vigorously. When she saw the Hardys and Chet, she called out, "Hello there! I'm Mrs Thompson. Can I help you?"

"Yes, thank you," Frank answered. "Is this Rim Road? We're looking for Captain Maguire's place."

The woman, who wore a faded but neat cotton dress, came closer and looked intently into the boys' faces.

"Maguire? Straight up to the top of the road. He lives in the last house—right on the edge of Black Hollow." As she answered, Mrs Thompson gave the boys another searching look.

Chet had turned towards the child, who was still weeping. "Poor boy," he said sympathetically. "Mind if I give him a bar of chocolate, Mrs Thompson?"

"Go ahead. Won't do any good, though. His dog disappeared last night, and nothing anybody can do is going to make him feel any better."

"That's a shame," said Chet. "Maybe if we keep an eye out, we'll see it, Mrs Thompson. What kind of dog?"

"Little brown creature," she answered. "He's got one white ear, and a collar, and a tag with his name, Skippy, on it."

"We'll look for him." As the boys turned to go, they heard the woman say sternly, "Bobby, you stop a-wailin'".

and go on into the house, now." Then she called to the boys:

"Wait!"

Surprised, the three turned back. Mrs Thompson came to the gate and began to speak in a low, intense voice.

"You seem such nice boys I just have to tell you something. Don't go near Black Hollow!"

"But why not, Mrs Thompson?" asked Frank.

"It's haunted—by the hex. Witch, I s'pose you'd call her. Two hundred years ago there was a pretty young woman around here that became a hex. She put spells on the dogs, and they disappeared and died. Then, by and by, people started to sicken and die, too."

"But couldn't they do anything about her?" asked Chet with unbelieving eyes.

"They tried to. They caught her and thought she'd stop castin' her spells. But she just stayed scornful and silent. One day she got away and vanished down in the hollow. But at night she used to come up and roam around, and dry up cows, and kill dogs, and at dawn folks would see her going back down into the hollow. Then one night came an awful, terrible screaming from the hollow. In the morning, when some brave men went down, there was a great scorched hole in the earth!"

"W-w-what happened?" asked Chet.

"Folks figured that Satan, the devil himself, came and got the witch and dragged her down to the centre of the earth!

"Then," added the woman, emphasizing her words, "a hundred years later, dogs started disappearin' again. They heard the hex screamin' at night in the hollow. Soon it all stopped again. But, now listen, boys. Another hundred years have gone by. The dogs are disappearin' again. *And at night we hear the witch screamin' in Black Hollow!*"

Peering at the trio closely, the woman saw that Chet Morton looked white. But in the eyes of Frank and Joe Hardy there was only a twinkle of amusement and disbelief.

Abruptly the woman shrugged her shoulders. "Don't say I didn't warn you!" With that, she turned and went into the house.

· 2 ·

A Midnight Scare

"Boy, that woman gave me the creeps." Chet shuddered, as the car ground up the hill in low gear.

"Relax," Joe told him. "You said yourself that people don't believe in that hex stuff any more."

"I don't know—round here they might," Chet continued in a worried voice. "All these thick woods, and hardly any houses. Do you suppose she's just making it up? After all, somebody—or something—must have taken Bobby's dog!"

Joe chuckled. "That's how these stories get started," he explained unconcernedly. "Something mysterious happens, and instead of looking for a sensible explanation, superstitious people think of spells and witches right away."

"I don't know," Frank put in thoughtfully. "There's the screaming, Joe. Mrs Thompson wouldn't have told us about that if she hadn't heard it herself."

A freshly painted letter-box, with the name T. MAGUIRE carefully printed on it, was the first thing the boys saw when they reached the top of the hill.

Beyond was a small grassy clearing. Both sides were bordered by woods made up of thickly leaved hardwoods and spruce trees. A neat rustic cabin, built of stripped logs pointed with white mortar, stood to their right. The polished headlights and radiator of an old car peeped from behind the little building.

"That's Captain Maguire's car, all right." Joe laughed. "It's fifteen years old, but he keeps it looking like new—just the way I saw it last."

The Hardys and Chet found, to their astonishment, that just beyond the rear of the house the ground dropped off into space. The lush grass gave way to smooth grey rock that fell steeply and disappeared in the tangled woods of a deep, cup-shaped valley below. For miles, the lip of rock curved round in a huge circle like the rim of a great bowl, broken here and there by a strip of green indicating a trail into the valley.

"This must be Black Hollow," Frank said quietly. "Funny, even the trees down there look black, though it's still daylight."

"Well, what do you say we get settled?" Joe suggested cheerfully. "Strange that Captain Maguire hasn't come out to meet us. Captain Maguire!" he shouted towards the cabin. "It's Frank and Joe Hardy! We've arrived!"

But the trim little house and the woods round it remained silent. Since they had written to the captain to say they were coming, the boys were surprised. They mounted the porch and knocked at the cabin door.

"No answer," said Joe, perplexed. "May as well try the door."

It was unlocked, so the visitors entered. They found themselves in a small, but neat and comfortable room, with a narrow bunk on one side. There was no sign of the captain. Chet Morton, venturing into the little kitchen beyond, suddenly called out.

"Whoops! A fellow could go swimming in here!"

Frank and Joe raced in. Their friend was standing in a large pool of water on the floor. Otherwise, the kitchen was spick and span: the pots on the wall hooks gleamed; the curtains were spotless. Everything was in its proper place.

Joe could not help chuckling. "Water on the floor? That's surprising. Captain Maguire's a tidier house-keeper than some women."

"Well, there's a leak in his plumbing somewhere," Chet complained ruefully. "My brand-new moccasins will be soaked! And this water's *cold*."

"That's because it's ice water, Chet." Frank stooped down before an old-fashioned icebox in one corner. He drew from underneath it a basin so full that the water was constantly overflowing to add to the pool on the floor.

Chet grinned. "An old-time refrigerator," Frank explained briefly. "The cake of ice inside melts and, the water has to go some place. Well, I'd drill a hole through the floor."

Joe frowned. "I wonder why Captain Maguire didn't empty this!" He picked up the basin and poured the water into the sink.

Frank nodded. "It's strange. The captain hates a mess. He'd be sure to come back and empty the ice-box basin, unless something unexpected detained him!"

"The bunk's unmade, too," Joe observed thought-fully. "That's not like him, either."

"It looks as if Captain Maguire left in a hurry," Chet summed up.

Suddenly apprehensive, the boys hurried out into the clearing again. Striding to the rim of the hollow, Frank cupped his hands and shouted:

"Cap-tain Maguire! Cap-tain Ma-guire!"

The boys strained to listen, but no answering sound came up from the dark hollow, not even an echo.

"We'll have to look for him," determined Frank. "He may be nearby, lying injured. I'll take the woods on this side of the cabin. Joe, you and Chet comb the other side. Keep calling for him while you search!"

Accordingly, Joe and Chet plunged into the woods together. The big trees which blocked the twilight, choked much of the undergrowth, making the going easy. Gradually they ceased to hear Frank's calls. The shadow under the trees deepened to dusky gloom. In another half hour it would be dark.

"It's almost night," observed Chet. "My stomach tells me it's long after suppertime and we aren't getting anywhere here. Let's go back!"

When they reached the clearing again, Joe called his brother. No answer came.

"Oh-h," moaned Chet in despair. "First no Captain Maguire. Now Frank's gone too."

"Hush!" Joe stopped him. "What's that?"

By now it was almost fully dark in the clearing. From the woods came a crackling sound of something moving.

"Joe? Chet?" came a familiar voice that caused Chet to sigh with relief. In a moment Frank had rejoined them.

"No sign of the captain," he reported briefly. "I did find a trail down into the hollow, though, and went along it a good way. That's what took so long. But I didn't see any trace of him there, either."

"It's a real mystery," agreed Joe, shaking his head. "But we've solved a few tough ones before. Let's get our gear inside. We can't do anything more out here."

Soon the delicious aroma of frying bacon and baked beans filled the tiny cabin. While Chet Morton tucked away a few extra helpings of each, Frank and Joe sat with him at the kitchen table and discussed the Maguire situation.

"The door wasn't locked and his car is in the yard," mused Frank. "That leaves a couple of possibilities."

"Yes. Either somebody else drove him, or he walked," Joe deduced. "Now why would he walk? Perhaps because he was going somewhere his car couldn't go."

"Into the hollow!" Frank exclaimed. "I was thinking that myself."

At this moment Chet Morton finished his supper. "Look, fellows," he volunteered, "I know how absorbed you two get in mysteries, so I'll wash the dishes while you look for clues, but on one condition."

"What's that, Chet?"

"You two get me some firewood for the stove."

"It's a deal!" The brothers laughed, and went outdoors to the captain's woodpile. They soon returned with armloads of kindling.

While Chet worked the hand pump to get some water, the two young detectives started their search for clues.

"Here's something," called Joe from the living-room. "I believe there's a shotgun or rifle missing from the captain's gun-rack. It has one empty space."

Frank had found something he thought was even more significant in the drawer of the kitchen table.

"Come here, Joe," he urged. The blond-haired boy found his brother poring over an ordinary kitchen calendar showing the dates for the previous two months.

"On certain days," Frank explained, "Captain Maguire has written the name of a breed of dog, and the name of an owner. See this one for June 10. 'Border terrier. J. Brewer, owner.' "

"You're right," admitted Joe, taking up the calendar. "But wait! On some dates there's another notation. 'She screamed.' "

"Screamed!" repeated Chet, who was washing the dishes. "Who screamed? The witch? Oh, great! I'd forgotten all about her! Did Captain Maguire hear her, too?"

"Could be, Chet," Frank answered seriously. "And the notations about the dogs—according to the story, the witch was a dog-killer, remember?"

"Say, what about that kid, Bobby Thompson, who was crying?" Chet broke in. "Is his name down there?"

Quickly Frank checked. "No, and that happened only last night. I wonder if that means Captain Maguire wasn't here last night and maybe all of today?"

"Possibly," Joe answered. "My hunch is that this witch-and-dog business was what Captain Maguire wanted to see Dad about!"

"Could be," Frank agreed. "And I'm afraid he's met with trouble. We'll start a search for him tomorrow as soon as it's light enough."

"Which means we'd better turn in and get some sleep." Chet yawned. "Well fellows, shall we flip coins to see who gets the bunk?"

"You take it, Chet." Joe laughed. "Frank and I will spread our sleeping bags on the floor."

The bright oil-filled lamps with their constant, gentle roaring sound were turned off. Their mantles glowed orange for a moment, then the cabin was silent and dark. Weary from the long drive and the evening's activities, the boys slept soundly.

But in the middle of the night they were rudely awakened by a fearsome sound. The three campers lay rigid, with eyes wide open, waiting tensely for the sound to be repeated.

Abruptly it came. The night outside was rent by a long, full-throated scream—like that of a woman in terror. It seemed to come from the depths of the hollow behind the cabin.

As the scream died away, Chet whispered, "Do you suppose Captain Maguire heard that last night and went to investigate?"

"I don't know," answered Frank, jumping up. "But a scream's a scream. It sounds as if someone is in danger. Slip on your shoes and clothes, and let's go!"

Minutes later, the trio, led by Frank, were hastening down the steep wooded path into the hollow. The boys' torch beams caused weird shadows to fall on the huge boulders and dense bushes. Tree roots and small protruding rocks made the unfamiliar path tricky and dangerous.

They saw no one, and finally their progress was barred by a rushing mountain torrent.

"This is as far as I got earlier!" Frank shouted above the sound of the water. "Guess we'll have to risk it now."

"Let's go!" Joe forged ahead into the stream.

The crashing white water exploded against the boy's body. The impact caught him off balance. Frank and Chet, following his progress with their torch beams, saw him stagger then go down underneath the relentless, rushing cascade!

·3·

An Eerie Trail

"DON'T lose sight of Joe! Keep both beams trained on him!"

With these words, Frank Hardy thrust his torch into Chet Morgan's hands. Then he plunged into the boiling torrent himself.

The freezing water crashed against his hips with a tremendous force. Joe, apparently unconscious, already had been carried several feet downstream. Cautiously Frank inched across, groping for footholds on the treacherous bottom.

"Better to move slowly than to risk a fall now!" he thought.

In a moment, guided by Chet's torches Frank reached his brother. He was lying unconscious against a rock; his head just out of reach of the water.

Frank braced his feet carefully and stooped. In a moment he straightened up, with Joe's limp form held firmly across his shoulders in a fireman's lift.

"Over here, Frank!" Chet called anxiously, lighting the way.

Frank lurched through the raging water to the bank, where Chet helped lower Joe gently to the ground.

"Is—is he breathing?" gulped Chet, who was pulling off his shirt to use as a towel.

"He'll be all right. Nasty crack on the head, that's all," Frank answered tersely.

He indicated a blood mark on Joe's temple. Then he swiftly stripped off his brother's soaking clothes. Meanwhile, Chet rubbed Joe's body briskly with his big woollen shirt.

In a moment Joe was blinking in the glare of their torches, and grinning weakly into their anxious faces. "Say, take the light out of a fellow's face," he protested feebly. "And what have you two done with my clothes?"

Chet took charge. "Never mind your clothes. Just put that shirt on to keep yourself warm. You Hardys are going straight back to the cabin to dry out by the stove. Whoever was doing the screaming down here can wait until tomorrow."

There was no more screaming during the night. In the morning, sunshine had already flooded the little clearing before any sign of activity was to be seen round the captain's cabin.

Inside, Frank and Joe were still sleeping soundly. From the kitchen came the clink and rattle of dishes and the unmistakable aroma of pancakes and sausages.

Clang! Clang! Chet Morton appeared in the doorway pounding on a metal pan with a big wooden spoon. "Breakfast, gang! Up and at 'em! It's almost ten o'clock!"

On the floor, two khaki sleeping bags stirred. Two heads popped into view.

"Oh-h-h—my aching head," Joe moaned and sat up. "Captain Maguire hasn't shown up, has he, Chet?"

"Ain't nobody here but us pancakes," the stout boy replied cheerfully as he re-entered the kitchen. "And if you two don't get a move on there won't be any of us pancakes—or sausages—left for long, either!"

Chet's threat was enough for the Hardys. They were ravenous after their exertions of the night before and wasted no time getting to the breakfast table. In half an hour the trio were refreshed and ready for a thorough search of Black Hollow.

Before starting, Frank slung the leather case containing his powerful binoculars round his neck.

"I'm taking these, just in case."

Frank led the way down the steep, twisting path while Joe brought up the rear. Once they were under the huge, closely growing trees, very little of the bright sunlight above filtered down to them. The dark, sombre evergreens made an almost impenetrable umbrella over their heads. All the time they kept looking for signs of Captain Maguire.

"It's easy to figure how this place got the name Black Hollow," Joe remarked.

The absence of wind in the well-protected valley made an unnatural stillness. Not a leaf stirred, and no small animals seemed to be moving. Joe's voice had a peculiar loudness and made all three a bit uneasy.

"Wait!" Chet Morton halted abruptly. "What's that?" All three listened intently. At the same time, their eyes surveyed the surrounding woods.

"Just the call of a crow," Joe said sheepishly. "Must be a mile away, at least."

When the trekkers reached the rushing torrent, Joe unslung the coil of stout Manila rope from his shoulder. Working rapidly, the brothers rigged a life-line for future passages by securing one end of the rope to a stout tree on the bank.

Once across, the search party continued their descent. Soon the sound of the turbulent stream was left behind. The eerie silence again surrounded them.

Once more Chet stopped. "Listen!"

"What now?" asked Joe with some impatience.

"I thought I heard something rustling."

"For Pete's sake!" Joe grinned at Chet. "It's your jeans' legs rubbing against each other. Come on! We'll never get to the bottom of this hollow."

The trio resumed its way down the trail.

"Hold it!" There was a tense note in Frank's voice.

"Hear anything?" Chet demanded eagerly.

Warily the alert youth's eyes scanned the trail behind them. "I just can't shake the queer feeling that somebody or something is following us."

"Must be stopping every time we do," muttered Joe. "I can't hear a thing."

After switching positions, the boys continued down the trail. Now it was Joe who scrambled forward in the lead. Frank, watching every tree and rock suspiciously, brought up the rear.

At last the steep path levelled off on to the floor of the hollow. Quickening his pace, Joe plunged forward. Before he knew it, his legs were caught by thorned branches. Innumerable tiny prickles bit through his jeans, grasped his sweater like claws, and dug into his exposed wrists and hands like fish hooks.

"Ow!" he shouted, struggling frantically. "What's got me?"

"You're in a brier patch," called his brother, laughing. "Simmer down. Stop fighting it. Go through it slowly. Take off one branch at a time."

By doing this Joe succeeded in freeing himself.

Carefully he worked his way through the patch, with Chet and Frank following. Suddenly he stopped once more.

"Frank! Chet!"

"What's the matter? Caught again?"

Grinning triumphantly, Joe turned to face his comrades. "Maybe I did rush in here without looking. But I wasn't the only one. Take a look at this!" With a flourish, he held up a piece of bright checked material about two inches square.

"It was clinging to this bush," he announced. "Looks like part of somebody's shirt. Maybe the captain's! It hasn't been here long. Not faded a bit by the weather."

"Let's see it," called Chet, struggling forward through the briers.

"Can't wait now," returned Joe as he emerged from the bushes. "Captain Maguire may be right near here!" He rushed headlong down the forest path, leaving Chet and Frank to catch up as soon as they could.

Just as they, too, worked clear of the tenacious thorns, another triumphant shout came from Joe, which caused them to set off at the double.

A wide, rock-strewn brook, apparently running the length of the valley, came into sight. Joe, kneeling beside it, was fishing something out of a little eddying pool on the near bank.

As Frank and Chet pounded up, he showed them an empty matchbook cover. It was wet, but still brightly coloured and fairly firm. "Hasn't been here long," he commented.

"It's a find all right," Frank agreed sombrely. "It

may not prove that Captain Maguire passed this way! But *some* human being did. Now let's follow the brook and keep our eyes open!"

The soft ground, covered with a brown carpet of pine needles, disclosed no footprints. But as Frank Hardy approached a large dead tree-trunk which had fallen directly across the path, his trained eyes picked out two distinct cup-like indentations in front of it.

At the same time, something shiny just off the trail attracted Joe's attention. Reaching in amongst the thick vegetation that grew beside the stream, he drew out a pair of empty shotgun shells!

"Must've been shot recently," he noted, sniffing. "I can still smell gunpowder."

Meanwhile, Frank carefully placed one of his knees in each of the sunken marks in front of the fallen tree.

"Whoever was here knelt in this spot and fired across the log," he concluded. "One of Captain Maguire's guns is missing. Maybe he fired the shots. But at what?"

"This trail is really getting hot!" Joe exclaimed, starting off.

The path continued to follow the bank of the brook. Suddenly Joe, in the lead, drew up to a sharp halt. "Hold it! On your guard! Prickles again! And hey, another piece of checked shirt material!"

"And that's not all," Frank broke in excitedly. "Look at the way these nettles have been crushed down in this one spot, as though something heavy had fallen on them!"

Now it was Chet's turn to make a discovery. With a yelp the stout boy bent over to snatch up a bent metal torch. Fragments of the shattered lens lay on the ground nearby.

"It's Captain Maguire's!" he declared excitedly, pointing out the initials T. M. scratched into the barrel of the torch.

Frank, in the meantime, had dropped down to examine the crushed nettle stalks more closely. "I'm afraid this is serious," he announced at last. "Some of these leaves are stained dark."

"Blood?" queried Chet in a worried tone, and the Hardys nodded.

At that moment the boys heard a slight noise just above them. Jerking their heads abruptly upwards, they were startled to see a face gazing down at them from the height of a boulder on the bank.

It was a strange, wild-looking, sun-browned face, framed with scraggly black hair. The fierce dark eyes glared at the watchers as the wide mouth shaped itself into a weird grimace.

·4·

The Windowless Cabin

THE Hardys and Chet stood frozen for a moment, as if entranced by the fierce stare of the wild face above them. Then suddenly the person behind the boulder was gone.

"The witch!" breathed Chet, who had turned chalk-white. "It must have got Captain Maguire!"

"Witch or no witch, it can't have gone far!" Joe cried out, leaping to his feet. "Come on!"

Frank sprinted forward with his brother along the forest path. The two boys ran through the dark woods, turning and twisting with the unfamiliar trail, dodging trees, and hurdling small bushes.

From up ahead came the sound of somebody crashing through the bushes. Suddenly Frank caught a glimpse of a tall, rangy figure in dark flannel trousers and green sweater, darting swiftly in and out amongst the huge trees.

"That's no witch." Frank panted. "But he sure can run!"

In fact, the long-legged stranger seemed to be pulling away from the Hardys, though they were both strong runners. Unexpectedly he cut sharply to his left, leaving the path and darting in a straight line across the forest floor. With amazing agility he leaped over fallen trees and ducked under low-hanging branches.

"Keep him in sight!" Joe yelled. "We'll trap him against the hillside!"

But the strange figure, upon reaching the steep, wooded side of the hollow, did not pause. Grasping at the small trees and bushes with his long arms, he clambered swiftly up the hillside from one foothold to another. Apparently he knew the route well.

Frank and Joe, meanwhile, were forced to waste precious time battling their way up. Doggedly they kept on, but the gap between the pursuers and their quarry widened.

At last, halfway up the valley wall, the man broke into the open on to the grey sunlit rock forming the upper rim of the hollow. Skilfully he moved diagonally from rock to rock until he disappeared from sight beyond the rim.

Frank and Joe, who had just emerged from the trees, sat down on a rock to catch their breath.

"There's one witch that doesn't need a broomstick," observed Joe, shaking his head ruefully.

Frank had removed his binoculars from the leather case hanging in front of him. He trained them on the rim of the valley where the strange figure had vanished.

Meanwhile, Chet had reached the side of the hollow. After a toiling climb the panting boy hove into view. "Whew! I thought I'd never catch up with you fellows. But old Chet wasn't going to stay down in those woods by himself. Say," he asked, looking round at the rocks apprehensively, "where's the—the guy with the face?"

"Escaped," Joe replied.

Frank, unable to spot the figure with his binoculars, moved up higher on the rock. He began to examine the entire perimeter of the little valley systematically.

By means of the glasses every fissure, every possible hiding-place in the rock rim could be studied. Nothing suspicious appeared beneath Frank's scrutiny. Finally he turned the glasses upon the floor of Black Hollow.

"See anything?" Joe called.

"Lots of trees, that's all."

As Frank continued to sweep the binoculars through a slow arc towards the end of the hollow, he was surprised to see a small clearing.

"Hold on—here's something!" he called down. Joe and Chet started upward.

"Well, what do you know about that!" declared Frank in an astonished voice, as Chet and Joe clambered up beside him. Silently he handed the glasses to his brother and pointed the direction with his finger. At first Joe saw only the little clearing at the edge of the trees.

"Look at the base of the rock wall," Frank said. "Look *very closely* at the pile of tree trunks and rocks you see there."

Wondering, Joe did so. Suddenly it occurred to him that the rocks and logs had been put together in a careful, regular manner.

"Why," he burst out, "that's not a pile at all. It's a little building! There aren't any windows, but I'd say it was a very cleverly camouflaged cabin."

"You're right, fellows," Chet agreed, when it came his turn to look. "Who would want to live in a place like that, anyway? Say, do you suppose it's the queer guy with the creepy face?"

"Could be," Joe answered. "Anyway, whoever lives there may be able to tell us where Captain Maguire is. Let's go and find out—right now."

"Aw, way down there to the end of the hollow? Have a heart, fellows. What about lunch?"

But Chet's protests fell on deaf ears. As the hungry boy knew from past experience, when the Hardy boys were following up a promising clue, ordinary things like lunch did not count!

Leaving the bright sunshine of the exposed rocks, the trio descended once more into the gloomy hollow. Frank and Joe quickly reached the forest floor.

As they waited for Chet, they heard a crashing sound from above and a familiar voice booming, "Help! Gangway!" As they jumped to one side, Chet came sliding down the steep hillside. He tumbled in a heap on the moss below.

"Jumpin' toads!" Joe exclaimed. "I thought the whole rock face was caving in on us!"

"Can I help it if I'm not made for these stupid mountains?" demanded Chet in an injured tone.

While Joe helped Chet get up, Frank scouted ahead to find the path once more. In a few minutes he located it.

"It isn't much of a trail any more," Frank reported. "But it's going in the direction we want."

Half an hour's walk brought them to the edge of the little clearing where Frank, raising his hand, signalled a halt. Even from there the mysterious little house was difficult to see, though it was not more than a dozen yards away.

Warily the boys scrutinized the clearing, as well as the odd house built of rocks and logs. It had a dark-brown door. Seeing no one, the boys stepped into the open, crossed the intervening space, and knocked boldly on the wooden door.

"Nobody home," muttered Joe as Frank knocked again and again. "I'm sure I heard something, though."

Chet, meanwhile, had poked his head round one corner of the log cabin. "Wonder what's fenced in over there?" he walked to the high palings of a strange three-sided enclosure.

"What do you see?" called Joe, as the stout boy peered through the fence.

"*Baa!*"

"There's your answer. Sheep!" Chet grinned. "Guess I scared 'em."

"Well, nobody's inside the house, that's certain," Frank concluded. "Let's take a look at the rest of the outside."

Accordingly, the three proceeded round the other side of the mysterious structure. Abruptly they found themselves face to face with the rock wall of the hollow. The strange little house had no fourth man-made side!

"Do you suppose whoever built this house was just lazy?" Joe wondered. "And used the rock for his wall? Or could there be some other reason?"

"The house certainly blends in with the rock," Frank reminded him. "You couldn't distinguish it from a distance without field glasses."

"We might as well head back," said Joe. "There isn't anything doing here. Personally, I'd like to find out who owns this house. In fact, it would be interesting to know who owns Black Hollow."

"Let's not forget Captain Maguire," Frank reminded them gravely. "This house and the person who was spying on us may or may not have something to do with his disappearance. Of one thing we *are* sure—

something happened to the captain here in the hollow. The sooner we get to town and report it to the sheriff, the better!"

An hour's vigorous hiking brought them back to Captain Maguire's cabin on the opposite rim of the hollow. While Chet grabbed a box of biscuits and three apples, Frank pencilled a brief note.

"For Captain Maguire—in case he comes back," Frank put at the top.

Joe and Chet said nothing. The three boys climbed into the yellow convertible and headed for the sheriff's office at Forestburg. All were convinced that the captain had met with trouble.

· 5 ·

A Reluctant Sheriff

EXPERTLY Frank piloted the yellow convertible down the steep, winding Rim Road. As it passed the Thompsons' house at the foot, the boys caught sight of little Bobby on the front porch, his chin in his hands.

"Poor kid," said Chet. "Reminds me, we haven't found any trace of his dog."

"Maybe the pup has come home," Joe suggested.

But Chet shook his head doubtfully. "Bobby wouldn't look as if he'd lost his best friend, and Skippy would be with him."

"You're probably right, Chet," Joe admitted. "Mrs Thompson said many other dogs have disappeared round here. I'll bet it's the work of an animal thief."

"But who would want to steal people's pets, and why?" demanded Chet, bewildered.

At this, Frank chuckled. "Mrs Thompson says the witch does it," he answered jokingly.

To Frank's surprise, his brother received his suggestion seriously. "I'm convinced there's a tie-in between the witch and these lost dogs," Joe stated. "Don't forget, Captain Maguire connected them in his calendar notations. It all fits the witch legend."

"Cut it out, Joe!" Chet protested nervously. "You don't believe that story?"

"No," Joe replied. "But I'll bet plenty of other people round here do. The Pennsylvania Dutch settled in many areas, even over here. They weren't really Dutch, but Germans, who came to our country between two and three hundred years ago for religious freedom. Anyhow, the old-timers brought some queer beliefs with them, such as the power of witches, charms, and spells. I've read that some of their descendants still hold on to these superstitions."

"Mrs Thompson does," Chet put in.

But Frank had already guessed what his brother was driving at. "Joe, do you think someone is deliberately trying to revive the witch legend by stealing dogs?"

"Yes. But don't ask me why."

The drive to Forestburg, through sparsely inhabited country and over narrow, twisting roads, took nearly two hours. Joe, a keen student of history, used the time to comment on the customs of people in Pennsylvania Dutch country. "After all," he reminded his companions, "a belief in witches wasn't uncommon. The Puritans in New England believed in them too, you know."

The car emerged from the hills on to the main street of Forestburg. On one side, the cross streets climbed steeply upward; on the other, behind substantial timber-built houses, ran a swift mountain river. An old stone mill stood by the water.

"That's where people brought their grain for grinding in the old days." Joe pointed out.

Another building, with the name GILLER'S GENERAL STORE on the window, attracted Chet's attention. Outside were coils of rope, shiny new tools, and sacks of feed.

"I'll get out here," the stout boy announced. "Somebody has to keep us in provisions while you two are busy with detective work!"

Frank parked, and Chet went into the general store. The Hardys proceeded down the street to the county courthouse, a trim, white wooden building, with round pillars supporting a wide porch in front.

The door to the county clerk's office pushed open under the pressure of Frank's knock. Inside, the boys could see a big, old-fashioned roll-top desk. Its many pigeonholes were stuffed with papers. The top of the desk, too, was littered; the various papers held down by four heavy metal paperweights.

"Hello?" Frank called. "Anyone in?"

In a moment a door at the back of the office opened. A friendly, middle-aged woman wearing glasses entered.

"Yes, boys? Mr Fry, the clerk, has gone out. May I help you?"

"We'd like to do some camping down in Black Hollow," Frank answered. "We want to find out the owner's name and ask his permission."

The woman, a native of the district, was able to answer the question without looking at the records.

"My goodness, that whole valley always belonged to the Donner family. But they've pretty much disappeared from round here. I don't know if there's any of 'em left now. The sheriff could tell you. He's across the hall."

Frank made a brief note of the name Donner. Then he and Joe thanked her and went out. Joe tapped on the glass of a door marked SHERIFF.

"Come in!" called a deep voice.

A short, heavy-set man, with a thick iron-grey moustache, was just replacing the receiver of his telephone. He seemed extremely busy. His waistcoat hung open, revealing colourful braces and his shirt sleeves were rolled up on his strong forearms. The sheriff turned in his swivel chair to face the Hardys, who quickly introduced themselves. They learned the official's name was Ecker.

"Well, what's on your minds?" he demanded.

Briefly, Frank and Joe related the facts of Captain Maguire's disappearance and expressed their fears for his safety. The sheriff listened with a preoccupied frown on his face and seemed scarcely to heed their story.

"What do you want me to do?" he asked when they had finished.

"We want someone to come and help us search Black Hollow, sir," Frank replied promptly.

Wearily the sheriff shook his head. "Too late to get any kind of party together today," he said. "I'll be mighty lucky if I can do anything about it tomorrow. All my men, regulars and special deputies, are tied up trying to catch that gang hijacking goods from inter-state trucks."

Frank and Joe looked at each other, thinking, "Dad's case?"

"There's no time to waste," Joe pleaded urgently. "Captain Maguire's life may be in danger!"

"Now take it easy, boys," the sheriff's gruff manner softened. "Maybe your friend just went for a hike alone. He might even be back in his cabin right now, waiting for you fellows. I can't pull my men off this other job without more evidence."

"But we found his torch!" Joe persisted. "And also

the shotgun shells, bloodstained leaves, and pieces of cloth!"

Sheriff Ecker sighed. "I just haven't the men today. I'll do my best to get a party together in the morning, but I won't promise."

"There must be *somebody* around who could help us!" Joe insisted.

Sheriff Ecker had already begun to study the report in front of him. Suddenly he looked up.

"Now that I think of it, there's Mr Donner, who lives down in the hollow all by himself. He must know every stone and bush in the place. His family has owned it since way back, y'see. He'll be very glad to help you boys, because that's the kind of man he is—always very friendly and helpful."

At this news the Hardy brothers exchanged a quick, puzzled look. "Did you say he lives in the hollow?" Frank asked.

"Yes. Don't know just where his cabin is, myself—never been there. But I guess you can find it."

Frank and Joe left the courthouse and found Chet waiting for them in the car. On the back seat were three big bags filled with groceries. "Found a nice place where we can have lunch," he announced cheerfully. "How'd you two make out?"

"Terrible," Joe replied flatly. "Sheriff's too busy to help us. Looks as if we're on our own. What do you think, Frank? Shall we call Dad? We can reach him through the New Jersey State Police headquarters."

"He might have some suggestions," Frank agreed.

"If you're thinking of telephoning," Chet put in importantly, "better listen to me first. I found out a few things about this town. Know who the biggest gossip in Forestburg is? Mrs Giller, the wife of the owner of the general store. Know who the local telephone operator is? Mrs Giller. Anything confidential you have to say to your father will be heard by Mrs Giller."

"I get you," Joe said. "There's not much Dad could do right away, anyhow," he added. "And at least we ought to give the sheriff a chance to come through with a search party. If that doesn't work out, then we can see what Dad suggests."

"Right." Frank nodded. "We'll wait till morning. If no searchers arrive, we'll hunt up this Mr Donner."

"Do you suppose he lives in the queer little house?" Joe asked.

"Could be," Frank answered. "We didn't see any other cabin through the field glasses."

Frank had started the car and he followed Chet's directions to a café. It proved to be an excellent eating place. Hot, juicy hamburgers and milk soon revived the boys' energy. Frank spoke with optimism.

"I've been thinking about the search," he told the others. "I have an idea for going ahead on our own."

Eagerly Joe and Chet gave him their attention.

"We're going to an animal auction," Frank announced.

"An animal auction!" Joe echoed. "Where?"

"On the outskirts of the next town. I saw the advertisement in the window of Giller's store as we went by. The auction is being held today, and ought to be starting in half an hour."

"But what are we going to buy?" Chet wanted to know. "Not an animal!"

"We sure are—a dog," Frank answered. "A dog to

"We're going to crash through!" Chet yelled

bait a trap. We'll take him back to Captain Maguire's cabin. If somebody's been stealing dogs, I just hope he tries to take ours, because we're going to be ready for him!"

"Great idea!" Joe said enthusiastically.

"Well, okay," agreed Chet doubtfully, "as long as we're careful. I'd hate to see harm come to any dog."

"Don't worry, Chet," Frank assured him. "We'll be on guard."

A few minutes later the boys started off once more. As they left the tiny village, the ride became increasingly bumpy.

"Wow!" Joe exclaimed. "This sure is a washboard road. Must've been built in horse-and-buggy days."

Recent heavy rains had gullied the road bed and left large exposed stones that pounded the tyres unmercifully.

After descending a long hill in a series of hairpin turns, the car approached a small iron-railing bridge across a deep chasm. The waters of an overfull mountain river churned below. A sign at the bridge read:

CAPACITY LOAD 5 TONS

"Guess you'll have to swim over, Chet," Frank said jokingly.

The plump boy snorted indignantly as the big convertible rolled on to the planks of the bridge. When it was halfway across, a splintering, cracking sound gave warning that the wooden planks were giving way!

"We're going to crash through!" Chet yelled.

·6·

Unusual Bait

As Frank Hardy heard the crunching sound of the planks collapsing beneath the car, the thought flashed through his mind: "Keep going! It's our only chance!" Instantly he pushed the accelerator pedal to the floor.

There was a whine of rubber on wood and a splintering sound. The back end of the convertible seemed to shudder and sink. Then at the last second the spinning tyres caught hold. The convertible lurched forward and was out of danger on the other side of the bridge.

"Whew!" exclaimed Frank, stopping the car. "What did I tell you, Chet? We should have let you cross the bridge yourself!"

But Chet was too thankful for their narrow escape to retort. Joe was already out of the car. "Let's have a look round," he urged.

Firmly taking hold of the iron railings, the brothers ventured out on to the bridge. Two planks dangled towards the dark water, and one was missing entirely.

"We'll have to do something," Joe declared, "to warn other drivers."

Crossing to the opposite bank, Frank and Joe set up a temporary road block by rolling some logs down from the wooded hillside. Meanwhile, Chet arranged a line of good-sized rocks to close off the bridge on the other end.

46

"We must report this as soon as we come to a phone," Joe remarked.

For more than a mile the road continued through wooded hills. At last the boys reached a farmhouse. On the letter-box was the name Wynn. Frank explained the situation at the bridge to the family, who had just sat down to a meal. Immediately the father left the table to phone the police.

"Such a narrow escape, boys!" the mother declared sympathetically. "Won't you sit awhile and eat something with us?"

Frank answered courteously, "Thanks a lot, Mrs Wynn. But we want to make the animal auction in town before it closes."

The boys said goodbye to the friendly family and resumed their trip. Fifteen minutes later they passed a large sign:

ANIMAL AUCTION
Just Ahead on the Right

In a moment Frank had pulled into a parking area next to several red buildings and pens. The trio jumped from the car and entered a high building with ramps of seats rising steeply to the roof. Men in working clothes occupied the seats, and from a platform at one end of the building a skinny man in waistcoat and shirt sleeves was speaking in a loud, ringing voice.

The auctioneer was showing his audience the good points of a young work horse. Next, the assistant led out a brown-and-white heifer.

"These are the larger animals," Frank observed. "The dogs must be in another building."

Frank, Joe, and Chet made their way to the door.

Suddenly Joe clutched his brother's arm. Without speaking, he pointed up into the tiers of seats. Amongst the farmers and stockmen sat a tall man with alert, piercing eyes and a full moustache. He wore a wide-brimmed hat, and a well-cut sports jacket.

"Don't you recognize him?" Joe insisted.

For a moment all three boys stared up at the tall, commanding figure. Suddenly the man's sharp eyes encountered their own. Feeling that they had embarrassed the man by staring at him, the boys went outside.

"That was Colonel Thunder, the puma trainer at Klatch's Carnival!" declared Joe. "What's he doing at an auction of domestic animals?"

"Search me," Chet answered. "Let's try here!"

He led the way into a long, low building filled with assorted sounds. Chickens cheeped, dogs barked, pigs squealed, goats and lambs bleated. The long-eared rabbits hopped about in cages, watching the commotion with twitching noses.

The dogs, mostly working and hunting breeds, were at the end of the room. Chet passed the collies that might be used for herding, and headed for the hounds, with their long ears and soft, expressive eyes.

"Always wanted a good hound dog!" he said enthusiastically. "Let's see. What shall we get? Coon hound? No—too big. Bloodhound? Too gloomy. Basset? Too fat, and its legs are too short."

"Look who's talking," Joe teased.

But Chet was too busy to hear. "Say, will you look at that, fellows?" He pointed.

In one corner stood a boy about eleven years old. Six fat, half-grown puppies were scrambling round his legs.

"Beagles," Chet commented, indicating the broad backs, short legs, and pointed tails.

Suddenly one of the pups bounded across the floor and began to nuzzle Chet's trouser leg. As the boy bent down, the beagle's long red tongue licked his hand frantically.

"This has to be the one," Chet declared happily, lifting the pup in his arms. "Come here, little fellow!"

"We'll take him," said Frank to the young owner. "How much?"

"Five dollars," the boy replied.

"Sold," agreed Frank, and took out his wallet.

As he selected a note, his attention was distracted by his brother, who quietly touched his elbow. With a nod, Joe indicated a transaction taking place a few stalls away. The man they had seen in the other building, Colonel Thunder, seemed to be buying a sheep.

"Friend of yours?" asked the boy with the pups.

"No. We've just seen him some place before."

"Well, he's getting cheated." The boy sniggered. "That sheep's so old it can hardly stand on its legs. Why would anybody buy an animal like that?"

"Just what I'm wondering," Joe murmured, as the boys walked out with their puppy. "Why does Colonel Thunder need a sheep? To feed his pumas?"

Once in the car, the little beagle began to tremble violently. "He'll be all right," Chet assured them. "Just the first time he's been away from his brothers and sisters." Kind-hearted Chet allowed the new pet to snuggle up inside his sweater.

As Frank started the car he said, "I want to get back to the cabin. There's just a chance Captain Maguire may have returned."

They had travelled a few miles over the bumpy road when Frank suddenly stopped the car and exclaimed in annoyance. "What's the matter with me? We can't go back this way! The bridge is out!"

"We'll have to find another route to Black Hollow," Joe said.

After turning round in a farm lane, Frank consulted the road map for a few minutes. Then he headed back towards the auction. At the next town the boys stopped to eat. As they set off again, the roads improved. It was now about seven o'clock. The sun was still high, but the air was pleasantly cool. Traffic became increasingly heavy. Many cars were filled with entire families, all going in the same direction.

"I wonder where these people are headed," mused Joe. "Most of them are dressed up."

"There's your answer," returned his brother.

Just ahead of them beside the road appeared a familiar line of tents. Soon the wind brought the sound of loud-speakers to their ears. "Klatch's Carnival has a new location," Frank observed.

"Good! Let's stop in," Chet proposed. "I could use some peanuts and popcorn!"

Frank looked sternly at their chunky friend from one side. Joe looked sternly at him from the other. "Aw, I was kidding, fellows," he said. "What I really want is to see that puma act again!"

"Well, that's better," Frank admitted. "I'd like to see it again myself."

After parking, the three friends made their way to Colonel Thunder's show tent. Chet carried the now-contented puppy inside his sweater. "I just thought of something," he said. "Do you suppose the colonel will be here? We just saw him at the auction."

"Don't worry," Joe answered. "He had time to get here while we were driving in the wrong direction."

Sure enough, the colonel's amazing act was already in progress when the trio entered. The tall trainer, wearing the same white outfit, managed the dangerous cats with the same daring disregard for the puma that remained always directly behind his back. This time, however, the performance went off without a hitch.

As the rest of the crowd climbed down from the tiered seats and filed out, Joe pushed forward to the cage for a closer look at the pumas. They were sleek beasts—young, strong, and well fed.

At this same moment Colonel Thunder emerged from the cage through a small door right next to Joe.

"Some animals you have there," Joe remarked to the man. "What kind of food do you give them to eat?"

"Raw meat that we get from local butchers," the colonel replied. He spoke politely, but his manner was distant, and he walked away immediately.

"But we saw him buying that sheep at the auction!" Joe protested as the boys drove homeward. "If it was to feed his pumas, why didn't he mention it?"

When Frank pulled up to the cabin it was almost nine o'clock. The sun was gone and the woods were dark, but overhead the sky remained luminous in the afterglow.

The boys, half hopeful that their host had returned, entered the cabin. But the place was silent. Frank's note lay undisturbed on the kitchen table. Captain Maguire had not returned.

"Where *is* he?" Joe burst out. "We *must* find him—and soon."

Suddenly Frank held up his hand. "Listen. Outside —a car!"

The boys ran to the door. In the clearing a car's parking lights gleamed. A plump little man in a business suit got out, slammed the car door, and walked rapidly towards them.

"Where's Maguire?" he demanded in an irritable voice that matched his rather dour face.

"Not here just now," Frank answered noncommittally.

"Not here! Where is he, then? He owes me some money!"

"I'll tell him you called," said Frank. "What is your name?"

"Webber—Wyckoff Webber— He knows. I'm an attorney in Forestburg."

"An attorney?" Joe spoke up. "Maybe you can tell us about Black Hollow, Mr Webber. It belongs to the Donners, doesn't it?"

"Yes. They used to have a summer cottage in it, but the place burned down. Haven't seen a Donner round here since."

"What do you make of the witch story?" Frank asked.

For a second the lawyer's eyes shifted away before he replied, "A lot of nonsense. The hollow has peculiar reverberating qualities. Somebody screaming miles away could be heard here, and clearly, too."

"I see. Well, we'll give Captain Maguire your message, Mr Webber."

As the lawyer's car pulled away, Joe observed, "There's one fellow I wouldn't trust for two minutes."

Chet now hurried to give their pet some milk and

meat scraps. As the little dog ate hungrily, Frank said, "I'm going to test out what Webber told us. Sounded phoney to me. I'll drive round to the opposite rim and yell. The wind is blowing in this direction. You fellows stay here and listen. When I get there I'll blink the car's headlights."

Frank drove off to circle round to the far side of Black Hollow.

·7·

The Hermit

Joe and Chet walked to the edge of Black Hollow. Darkness descended. Presently a short beam of light could be seen travelling rapidly along the opposite rim, almost two miles away.

"Must be Frank," Joe murmured as he raised his binoculars. For a moment the beam disappeared. Then the boys saw two bright lights blink on and off.

"Frank has turned the car to face us," said Joe.

Chet and Joe held their breaths, listening intently. A fresh breeze blew against their faces from the direction of the car lights, but no sound reached them. In a moment the lights were gone and the beam could be seen travelling again. Frank was on his way back.

When he reached the cabin Frank said, "I screamed my lungs out. I blew the car horn, too."

"Didn't hear a thing," Joe told him as the boys re-entered the cabin. The oil-filled lamps were lit, and Chet prepared supper.

Frank rested his elbows on the table, frowning. "The hollow doesn't have any echoes to speak of," he noted, "so Webber was lying. Why?"

"Sure," said Joe. "He has lived round here long enough to know the truth. What's he hiding? Is he covering up for somebody?"

"He didn't seem to know that Captain Maguire is missing," Chet put in.

"I wouldn't be too sure of that," Joe cautioned. "He may have come round just to find out how much we know."

Frank agreed. "There's something more than witchery going on here. Things look bad for Captain Maguire. We must press the hunt for him tomorrow!"

Hoping to make an early start next day, the boys decided not to expose the puppy to the dog thief and stay on watch, but to get some sleep.

Sleep would not come, however, except in fitful dozes. Each boy found himself waiting, listening for the terrible scream that had roused them the night before.

About midnight, Joe whispered suddenly, "Hush!"

A new sound floated up from the depths of Black Hollow—a long, screeching sound.

"Creepers!" Chet quavered. "Last night the witch screamed. Tonight she's screeching. What next?"

Meanwhile, the little puppy had begun to whine and tremble.

Suddenly Joe began to laugh.

"I don't see what's so funny," Chet said crossly. "Our poor puppy is shaking all over!"

"Of course he is." Joe laughed. "He hears his natural enemy. Witch, my eye. That screeching, my friends, is nothing but the screech of an owl!"

"Owl?" repeated Chet. "A screech owl?"

"No. A screech owl wails, Chet," Joe replied. "It's the barn owl that screeches."

Chet sat up in his bunk. "You mean that what we heard tonight was nothing but a barn owl!"

Joe nodded. "It must have been. And barn owls have been associated with witches and ghosts for centuries. But that screaming last night definitely did not come from any barn owl."

"And furthermore," said Frank, "barn owls don't steal dogs. Well, let's get some sleep before the sun comes up. We'll just have to get used to these weird sounds."

"Owl, or no owl," Chet put in, "it gives me the willies!"

A grey, misty dawn the next morning found the boys already up and about. After breakfast, while Chet made sandwiches to take on the search, Frank and Joe walked out to Rim Road to look for Sheriff Ecker's party.

In an hour a bright sun had burned the mist away, but no searchers had arrived. "All right," said Frank. "We're on our own. We'll go down and call on this Mr Donner first."

The door of the cabin opened, and the little beagle rushed out, only to be brought to a tumbling halt by a piece of clothesline attached to his collar. Chet held the other end in his hand.

"Whoa there, Mystery!" called the stout boy, who carried a rucksack on his back.

"Mystery?" repeated Joe. "That his name?"

"Yes, because he's the little feller that's going to help us solve this mystery."

Once more the three boys descended the steep path to the floor of the hollow. Around them the woods preserved their eerie silence. Even the puppy showed no desire to roam about.

Suddenly Frank called a halt. "It's the same as

yesterday," he said in a low, perplexed voice. "I'm sure we're being followed!"

The three listened, hardly breathing. But there was nothing to be heard or seen. "All right. Let's go!" Frank signalled finally.

Almost before they knew it, the boys had reached the queer, windowless cabin. Frank stepped forward and rapped sharply on the door.

Immediately it was pulled inward. A tall, broad-shouldered man with heavy brows, a full moustache, and piercing eyes confronted them.

"Colonel Thunder!" Joe blurted.

"Colonel?" the man repeated quizzically in a deep, hearty voice. "Take it easy on the rank, there, boy. You couldn't even call me a private, seeing as how I was never in the army!"

"You mean," faltered Chet, "you're not Colonel Bill Thunder, the fearless animal trainer?"

The big man gave a booming laugh. "No. Afraid I'm just plain Walter Donner."

Perplexed, Joe stammered, "Well, Colonel Thun— I mean, Mr Donner—we're afraid that something has happened to a friend of ours, Captain Thomas Maguire —he owns a cabin on the other side of the hollow. He disappeared from his cabin at least two nights ago!"

Immediately Mr Donner's genial face became serious. "Hmm. Better come in awhile, boys. Just tie the puppy outside there, will you?"

Frank, Joe, and Chet followed their host into a tidy little room furnished with rustic wooden table and chairs. "Leave the door open for the light. Sit down here. I'll be back in a minute."

The tall man ducked easily through a low, narrow

doorway into the kitchen beyond. The boys could hear pans being moved about, and a door being closed. In a moment Donner was back.

"Now," he addressed them, "who is Captain Maguire, and what's happened to him? Let's get all the details."

The boys introduced themselves, then Joe explained. "He's a friend of ours who lives on the edge of the hollow. The captain was expecting us. When we arrived, day before yesterday, there was no sign of him. He'd vanished. We tracked him into the hollow, where we found his torch and two shotgun shells that he probably fired."

"Yes!" Donner broke in. "There *was* some shooting the other night. At first I thought it was a hunter. but I didn't hear any dogs, which are used for hunting coon, or anything legal. So I assumed it was somebody poaching deer. As for your friend, I'm sorry. I never heard of him."

"Well, thanks anyhow, Mr Donner," said Frank. "But say—would you know anything about the dogs we understand are disappearing in the neighbourhood? We promised to look out for a puppy that's missing."

Thoughtfully, the big man frowned. "Very likely a dog thief. You see, there's a big illegal market on dogs for medical experiments. I'd like to get my hands on the wretch who steals them," he added indignantly. "You see, I like animals!"

"We did see something else suspicious, yesterday," Frank went on. "A strange person spying on us. He looked—well, he seemed half wild."

"There I can help you," declared Mr Donner, raising his finger. "You must mean Simon. He's a mute boy who lives with his widowed mother over in the next valley. He can hear, but he lost his voice by an injury to his throat, I understand, even before he learned to talk. He runs wild in the hollow all summer. Lives on berries and whatever he can pilfer from nearby farms."

"Is he dangerous?" Chet asked.

"Mmm—I'd keep away from him. He'd just as soon heave a rock at you as not. You know, it might be Simon who is making off with these dogs. Animals and birds seem to interest him."

"Brr," Chet shuddered. "I don't see how you stand it here, Mr Donner. Boys running half wild—the witch shrieking at night."

At this their host's eyes twinkled with amusement. "Well, young fellow," he said to Chet with a wink, "intelligence tells me it's certainly no witch. But I'll have to admit every time I hear the screams, chills run up and down my spine!"

Frank and Joe, thinking how they had been startled by the owl, grinned also. A soft popping sound was heard from the kitchen.

"There's my coffee," Donner announced abruptly. "Come into the kitchen, boys."

With eager curiosity Frank, Joe, and Chet followed their host through the narrow doorway. They found themselves in a small windowless kitchen lit by two oil-lamps. There was a little wood stove for warmth, but Donner cooked on a small range. In a moment he had poured out coffee for them.

"Yes, I camp out here," he said, as the four sat round the plank table near a ventilation flue. "I come for a rest. I take it easy, and raise a few sheep. It's a quiet place."

"Quiet is right," Chet agreed. "You'd never know it was here!"

"Ah, but that was the idea," said Donner. "The idea of living in the cabin, I mean. I guess you could call me a hermit.

"I love this cabin. You notice the way it blends with the surroundings? Take a look at the back wall of this kitchen. See? Solid rock. That's the rock face of the hollow. This cabin is over a hundred years old. Do you know what was going on then?"

"Let me see," said Joe. "That would be just about the time of the Civil War."

"Right. This was one of the stations on the Underground Railway—the route for smuggling runaway slaves up to Canada. That's why it's so well hidden, and has no windows, no lights to give it away at night. It's small, but comfortable."

While he examined the unusual little house, one fact stuck in Joe's mind: There seemed to be only one door in the place; the one at the front. How was a runaway slave supposed to escape if he were surprised here? Besides, hadn't he heard a door closing earlier, or had he imagined it?

While Joe wondered, suddenly there came an urgent knocking.

·8·

Rock Barrage

THE sunlight streaming into the hermit's cabin was suddenly blocked off by the stocky figure of Sheriff Ecker.

"'Morning, Donner," he said, as the tall man came forward with hand outstretched. "Sorry to break in, but we're going to need your help."

By this time Frank, Joe and Chet had come from the kitchen. "Oh, the boys found you first, did they?" The sheriff spoke in a gruff but friendly voice. Three men were standing behind him.

"Well, here's your search party," Ecker said to Joe. "It's not much of a posse—three men are all I can spare, but we'll do what we can. With you fellows and Mr Donner here, we'll have eight, and that's pretty good. Sorry I couldn't get hold of a good dog to take along."

"That's all right, Sheriff," Chet spoke up. "We have Mystery!"

"Our beagle," Joe explained hastily.

"Search party?" repeated Donner. "That sounds terribly official to me, Sheriff!"

Sheriff shot a quick look at the smiling Donner. "Did the boys tell you what's up?"

"Well, they *did* say something about their captain friend being missing. He probably just went for a long hike in the woods. I'd no idea it was so important that the sheriff personally would lead a search party in these out-of-the-way parts," he added, smiling.

Sheriff Ecker frowned, obviously reminded of other urgent matters. Joe and Frank glanced at each other—would the man change his mind about conducting the search? But Ecker merely said:

"I'd like you to come along, Mr Donner, since you know the hollow so well."

"By all means," agreed the big man. "But now that you are here, come in and have a look at my little retreat, Sheriff. It's over a hundred years old. I was just telling the boys that it used to be a hide-out for runaway slaves."

Hospitably, Donner conducted Ecker through the cabin, while the boys waited. Joe went to introduce himself to the three deputies.

Chet, meanwhile, accompanied by the frisky young puppy, wandered over to the three-cornered sheep pen and peered inside. Frank stayed near the door of Donner's house. He stared thoughtfully at the ground. Something shiny that lay deep in the tall meadow grass caught his eye. Unobserved by the others, he stooped down, examined the object, and slipped it into his pocket, just before Donner and the sheriff appeared.

"Ready to go, boys?" Donner boomed.

The group now formed under his direction. Donner had put on a dapper felt hat with brightly-coloured trout flies hooked in the band. With an amused grin he was stuffing a long-barrelled target pistol with a fancy pearl handle into his belt.

"Never been a deputy before," he joked. Frank and Chet took their places with Joe.

"Now, my husky young friend," Donner went on, gripping Chet's shoulder, "suppose you come up front with your dog. Black Hollow has two kinds of terrain, woods on the bottom and rock on the sides. We'll take the woods first, and the rocks later."

Quickly the searchers were told by Sheriff Ecker to fan out in order to cover as much ground as possible. Each person was to keep the man to the right of him in plain sight, and be responsible for the area between them.

Chet, with Mystery eagerly sniffing and straining at his home-made leash, was placed near the centre, slightly in advance of the rest. Sheriff Ecker stationed himself on the left wing, and Frank and Joe had the extreme right. Donner took the middle, so he could call directions. In this order the party advanced into the thick woods on the hunt for Captain Maguire.

The tangled undergrowth, dim light, and the numerous trees growing densely together made progress difficult and slow.

"Sheriff!" Donner called out. "There's a little gully over near you. Check it. Maguire may have fallen into it."

In a minute the report came back, "Nobody there!"

Another time Donner sang out jokingly, "You— Joe Hardy—you'll be coming to a hollow tree. Better look and see if your friend's inside!"

Joe smiled faintly, but he was beginning to be annoyed at Donner's rather lighthearted approach to the affair. "Treats the whole thing like a lark," the young sleuth thought.

All the while his keen eyes scanned the ground, bushes, and heavy undergrowth. Frank and Chet also were constantly on the alert.

The search continued through the gloomy hollow. All at once, Mystery gave a high-pitched yap at something that had startled him.

"A man!" Chet shouted. "I see a body!"

From both sides the searchers came pounding towards him. All stared into the dark woods. Ahead lay the huddled figure of a man in black coat and cap, and grey trousers!

Tensely, with Mystery bounding along, they pressed forward. Frank and Joe were the first to reach the figure. Both gasped in relief.

"It's only a fallen tree limb!" Joe exclaimed, as the others came up.

"Some eyes you've got, Morton," Donner roared. The deputies shook their heads in a half-amused, half-exasperated gesture.

"Well, it *looked* like a body—from far away," Chet apologized ruefully.

"Might as well call a halt and rest now that we're all together," Sheriff Ecker interposed.

Eager to make amends, Chet opened his rucksack and passed round tuna-fish, egg-salad, and ham-and-cheese sandwiches. The three deputies sat down on the tree limb that had fooled Chet. Frank, Joe, and the sheriff squatted on their heels, while Donner lounged against a tree.

"It's noon, but you'd never know it in these dark woods," Sheriff Ecker commented.

While Chet went from man to man with a big Thermos of coffee, Frank brought a tiny transistor radio from his pocket and turned on the twelve o'clock news.

The swift, precise voice of an announcer roused the search party's attention:

"New Jersey and Pennsylvania State Police were forced to admit defeat this morning in their attempt to recover thousands of dollars' worth of surgical equipment stolen last night from a truck en route to New Jersey.

"Daring hijackers stopped the trailer carrying the equipment, knocked the driver unconscious, and apparently fled in a vehicle of their own. No trace of them has been discovered."

Frank and Joe exchanged meaningful glances. This news indicated their father's work on the case was far from finished!

"Officials emphasized," the announcer continued, "that this robbery was only the latest in a series of many which have taken place in the area recently. Combined efforts of police in both states to round up the hijackers have so far ended in total failure."

"Turn it off," the sheriff snapped.

"Donner, however, merely chuckled and shook his head with amusement. "Now isn't that just like our State Police!" he said. "Just don't want to work overtime, probably. No wonder they can't keep up with these hijackers. When thieves are on a job they don't worry about the hours!

"Now, Sheriff, you tell me," the big man went on, "why aren't these criminals caught? All it would take, it seems to me, is a system of alerting all policemen within a reasonable radius, and posting them on all possible escape routes."

"Mr. Donner, I know you mean well," answered Ecker, frowning, "but you're hittin' kind of close to home. I was out all night myself, and my men too. We were out the night before that. I'd be watching the roads right now, if I wasn't here searching for this man who's disappeared. A policeman can't do two things at once, y'know—no more than another man."

"You're right, Sheriff, and I'm sorry," Walter Donner apologized. "Let's finish this search."

Accordingly, the party spread out in line again, and the hunt went on. By mid-afternoon the searchers had thoroughly combed the wooded valley floor without discovering a clue to Captain Maguire's whereabouts. Now they found themselves up against the steep, rocky side of the hollow.

"I see a cave up there," said Donner, pointing above to ledges and boulders. "It's just possible we may find something in it. You boys go on ahead. I'll come after you. I'm not in very good condition for climbing."

In a moment Joe Hardy was working his way nimbly up the grey rock wall. Frank and Chet followed close behind. Above them, the cave mouth was a black opening in the rocks.

Soon Joe reached a narrow cross ledge about a third of the way up. As he pulled himself on to it, however, he was suddenly staggered by a stone that crashed into his forehead.

"Look out! Above you!" Donner shouted.

Other stones came bouncing down at the climbing boys, narrowly missing them. Looking up, they saw a tall, lean figure at the top of the hollow. He kept hurling the dangerous missiles.

"It's Simon!" cried Donner. "Watch out!"

The mute boy waved his arms threateningly.

"He's trying to stop us from coming up," Joe said grimly. "Well, he's not going to succeed!"

Though his head was bleeding, the plucky boy

crawled upward again after Frank, who was now in the lead. Chet was climbing at a slower pace behind them. Seeing the trio advance, the strange boy redoubled his barrage.

One stone bruised Frank's forearm. Another skipped off his back. Dodging, the determined boy crawled steadily upward. He reached the ledge at the mouth of the cave, then he turned, and with a skilful pull and twist, hauled his brother up beside him.

Abruptly the stoning ceased. Frank and Joe turned to face the cave itself. The next instant they froze in their tracks. Barely three feet from their faces a deadly snake was coiling to strike!

At that moment two more of the venomous snakes slithered out of the cave itself!

· 9 ·

Setting a Trap

THERE was no escape for the Hardys—the ledge was two narrow. They were trapped by the deadly reptiles. The steep drop below the cave cut off all chance of rapid descent. While the two rattlers slithered towards their exposed ankles, Frank and Joe raised their arms in an attempt to ward off the strike of the reptile coiled just above them.

Crack! The shot of a pistol was followed in a split second by the unmistakable smack of a bullet hitting home. The snake's long body exploded straight upward, writhing, and then fell with a thud at the Hardy's feet. Startled, the two other rattlers retreated into the cave.

"Off the ledge, quick!" cried Frank.

Scrambling backwards, both boys hung for an instant by their fingertips from the ledge. In another moment they were grasped firmly by Chet Morton and Walter Donner, who had climbed up the steep rock face. Donner held in one hand the smoking, long-barrelled pistol which had ended the life of the deadly snake.

When the four climbers were back on the ground, Sheriff Ecker wiped his brow in relief. "A close call," he declared, still shaken. "Wasn't a thing *we* could do!"

68

"Lucky for us you decided to come up, Mr Donner," Joe addressed the tall man gratefully. "And even luckier you can shoot so well."

"We're certainly thankful you were near enough to shoot," Frank added. "Your bullet must have caught that rattler right in the head!"

Walter Donner's face, usually so good-natured, had become serious, and even stern.

"I'm glad I happened to be here," he answered. "I hate to think of what would have happened otherwise. Suppose you boys had gone rushing up to that cave, without looking where you were going, and I wasn't around? It would have been a terrible tragedy!".

Putting one arm around Chet's shoulders, and another round Joe, Donner continued, "If you ever listened to anything, listen to me now. You can't be too careful in the woods! You never know where danger is going to come from—sometimes under your feet, sometimes over your heads. Snakes like to sun themselves on dry, rocky ledges. Don't climb around carelessly. Once you *are* in open country—remember —caution, boys, always caution."

"Mr Donner," one of the deputies said emphatically, "I've got two boys at home, and I couldn't have said it better to 'em than you just did."

"Yep," another agreed. "The woods is no place for kid stuff. You've got to be on the lookout."

"It's true," Sheriff Ecker put in. "Most people who get in trouble in the woods just don't know any better. They can't tell directions, they're not careful where they step, and so on. Always somebody coming up from town and getting lost in these mountains."

"Well"—Donner's voice became jovial again—"I'm

sure these lads are going to be real careful after what happened today." He turned to the Hardys. "Maybe you'd better stay out of Black Hollow entirely. It's a dangerous place, especially with that Simon throwing rocks at people. Besides, it seems certain your friend isn't here."

Thwarted and disappointed at finding no trace of the missing captain, Frank, Joe, and Chet thanked the search party and returned to their cabin. Frank washed and dressed the cut on his brother's head.

"How's it feel?" he asked.

"Terrible—I have a corker of a headache."

While Joe lay down to rest, Frank again studied the calendar notations made by the captain. Chet Morton busied himself getting supper. When it was ready, the stout boy called out cheerily:

"Soup's on. Come and get it!"

Although Chet had outdone himself to produce a meal of steak, fried potatoes, and hot vegetables, the brothers hardly seemed to notice the food. They ate in thoughtful silence. Chet watched his two friends uneasily.

"Still feeling blue about it?" he asked at last.

"About what, Chet?"

"About that lecture Donner gave us. He sure made it sound as if we're babes in the woods. Boy, did that get me mad for a minute there! Why, the three of us have been camping for years. I felt like telling him a thing or two!"

"So did I, Chet," Joe admitted ruefully. "But I couldn't, because he'd just saved our lives. It really looked as if we *were* babes in the woods."

"Let's be fair, fellows," Frank put in. "It's true we're

not tenderfeet, but what happened was our own fault. We should have thought of the possibility of snakes. I know they're apt to be in rocks as well as Donner does. . . ."

A new idea suddenly crossed Frank's mind. ". . . as well as Donner does," he repeated thoughtfully. "If he knows it, why didn't he warn us before we went up? Besides, he knows more than that. He knows every rock and tree in Black Hollow, as Sheriff Ecker told us. We trusted Donner's knowledge of the hollow—that's why we weren't careful. But who sent us up to that cave? Donner!"

"That's right!" Joe chimed in excitedly. "And remember, he invited us to give up the search, and stay out of the hollow. There's something fishy about that man and his house. I know I heard a door open in the back. But there wasn't any sign of one in the kitchen."

"What I can't figure out," Frank went on, "is why Donner would send us up to a den of rattlers and then save our lives. Because the only reason he climbed up along with us was to get within pistol range of the snakes. The sheriff and his men couldn't shoot—we were in their line of fire."

"There's your answer," Joe declared forcefully, "I believe it was Donner's idea to establish us as woefully inexperienced in front of witnesses. Suppose some 'accident' does happen to us down there. The sheriff won't be suspicious, because he thinks we don't know how to take care of ourselves!"

"You mean Donner may be planning to kill us and make it look like an accident?" Chet asked.

"Who knows?" Frank nodded seriously. "Another

thing—the rock throwing by Simon, the mute. Is he in league with Donner? Or was he perhaps throwing stones at us because we were with Donner?"

Joe frowned "It's a puzzler, all right, including Donner's resemblance to Colonel Thunder."

"Hey—I nearly forgot!" Frank reached into his pocket and placed a shiny metal disc on the table.

"What's this?" asked Chet, picking it up. "Oh, a dog's name tag. What's it say? Skippy! That's Bobby Thompson's little dog! Where'd you find this?"

"In the grass near Donner's front door."

"You think Donner's been stealing dogs?" Joe queried. "Is *he* mixed up in some kind of animal racket? He said himself there was an illegal market for dogs."

Perplexed, Frank shook his head. "You have me there. If he steals them, I can't figure out what he does with them. There weren't any round his house."

"That's true," Chet agreed "I took another look in the sheep pen. Nothing in it but sheep. Could be that Skippy just wandered off from the Thompsons' and lost his tag down by Donner's."

At that moment the boys' own puppy could be heard noisily lapping up warm milk from a pan that Chet had put down for him.

"We can't let anything happen to Mystery!" Chet finished anxiously.

Hearing his name, the beagle romped happily over to Chet's chair. "Yes, Mystery," the chunky boy crooned, while the dog's tail thumped the floor, "we won't let anything happen to you!"

"All the same, I think tonight is the time to set our trap for the dog thief," Frank declared.

"Right," Joe agreed promptly. "Mystery, old pup, you're going to be the bait."

"Now wait a minute, fellows," Chet protested "I won't agree to this unless I'm sure we can safeguard Mystery!"

"I think we can," said Frank "We'll just tie him on the porch after dark. Chet and Joe—you watch from right inside the door at all times. I'll hide at the side of the house. That way, we ought to catch any dog thief that comes here!"

Accordingly, about ten o'clock, the oil-filled lamps were turned out, and the little cabin was in solid darkness. Heavy clouds, promising a storm later on, had begun rolling across the sky. The air was dense and still.

Chet and Joe opened the cabin door quietly, and led Mystery outside. After securing the dog's rope to the railing, the two withdrew to stand guard. From within they could scarcely make out the dog in the total darkness.

Soon afterwards Frank, wearing dark clothes, slipped out the back door and stationed himself between Captain Maguire's old car and the side of the cabin, a few steps from the porch.

The youth sat down and waited, listening intently. Gradually his eyes became accustomed to the night. Even so, he realized that a person advancing across the clearing against the backgound of thick trees would be nearly impossible to see.

The night air seemed to grow heavier and warmer. Flickers of lightning began to play about the horizon. The thunder became louder. Suddenly a streak of lightning lit up the clearing for an instant, then blackness closed down again. A tremendous thunderclap followed instantly. Frank checked his watch. It was nearly midnight.

Another flash came, accompanied by a long roll of thunder. On the porch the beagle whined.

"Storm's almost on top of us," Frank noted.

Almost immediately came another white blaze of lightning, and a fearful crash of thunder. The first heavy drops of rain pelted down. Mystery's whines suddenly changed to frantic, high-pitched barking.

Distracted for a moment by the storm's arrival, Frank hesitated a moment, then sprang forward. At the same time Joe and Chet burst out the front door.

Mystery was gone!

The dog's yelping could be heard, but the sound grew fainter. A sheet of lightning made the clearing and woods even brighter than day. Frank, Joe, and Chet caught sight of a figure fleeing swiftly down the path into the hollow.

"After him!" Joe shouted.

Armed with torches, the three boys raced in pursuit.

· 10 ·

Sketch of a Thief

SPRINTING across the clearing, Frank, Joe, and Chet entered the dark woods on a run. They were forced to slow up at once, however, in order to pick out the path with their torches.

Ahead of them, the dog thief pounded forward in the darkness, apparently certain of his way even without a light. Mystery's whimpers came back to the boys, then were drowned in a rumble of thunder. Raindrops could be heard pattering on the tree leaves overhead. In the momentary glare of lightning flashes, the three boys could see a figure running ahead swiftly downward towards the floor of the hollow.

Suddenly, from the blackness, came a human cry, followed by the clatter of something or somebody falling among the rocks, then a heavy crashing in the bushes. All the while Mystery barked frantically.

Recklessly the pursuers dashed to the bottom of the path. Someone was groaning in pain in the dense undergrowth to their right. The sound of running footsteps continued.

"Joe! Chet!" Frank commanded breathlessly. "Find out what's going on in the bushes. I'll keep after the thief!"

"Roger!" snapped Joe.

With torch beams darting here and there, Joe and Chet moved forward through the dense growth. The crashing of the bushes told them their quarry was moving, too. But no more groans reached their ears. Soon they could hear nothing but the sound of the rain falling heavily on the leaves, and the claps of thunder.

"No use. We've lost him," Joe decided quickly. "Back to the path, Chet."

In the meantime, Frank had been able to increase his speed on the level valley floor. Hoping to catch the fleeing figure off guard, the youth no longer used his torch, but relied instead on the lightning's vivid glare.

Suddenly, as the woods were illuminated by an especially dazzling flash, Frank recognized the tall, thin figure running just thirty yards ahead with a wriggling object under one arm. "Simon!" Frank called out. "Wait!"

But the strange boy turned and made a dash for the rocky side of the hollow.

Limping slightly as though hurt, but still with amazing agility, Simon clambered swiftly upwards over the rocks. Frank had almost closed the gap between them in a final spring. Bounding upwards himself, he made a lunge and grasped the fleeing boy's ankle firmly with one hand. Mystery, barking fiercely, was thrown clear. Simon, who had been dragged backward, suddenly recovered and threw himself upon Frank.

By now the storm was at its height. The rain fell in sheets. Flickers of lightning illuminated the fierce struggle between the two boys.

Keeping a cool head, Frank tried to subdue the

"Drop it, Simon!" shouted Joe

boy by means of a wrestling hold. But Simon's wet clothing and his unexpected, immense strength enabled him to wrench free, throwing Frank to the ground. Quickly Simon grabbed a heavy rock and poised it above Frank's head.

"Drop it!" came a sudden shout from below.

Startled, Simon turned and the rock slipped from his grasp. Frank quickly scrambled to his feet and dived forward to make a fast, clean tackle. In another moment Joe and Chet arrived and made the capture complete.

As Frank and Joe held on to the tall, mute boy, Chet demanded angrily, "Where's my dog?"

"Take it easy, Chet," Frank warned. "Simon's injured, and he's frightened. Remember, he can't answer you."

There was no need for Chet to hunt for Mystery. The drenched, trembling little beagle came leaping frantically and joyfully to his master.

"Get that piece of clothesline on Mystery's collar," Frank directed. "We'll tie Simon's hands for safety, until we get him back to the cabin."

Slowly the three friends and their captive made their way up out of the hollow. Frank and Joe supported the limping mute boy on either side as they climbed the steep trail. Simon made no further attempt to escape.

By the time the drenched boys reached the cabin the rain had stopped and a fresh wind was clearing away the storm clouds.

"Mission accomplished," Chet declared delightedly.

"Now for something to eat, and then a nice, dry bed. What d'you say, Mystery?"

After changing his clothes Chet went immediately to the kitchen. In a few moments he had a big pan of soup heating on the stove, then made ham sandwiches for everyone.

Meanwhile, Frank and Joe had untied their prisoner, told him to remove his wet clothing, and given him a warm bathrobe of Captain Maguire's to put on.

In the brightly lit cabin, Frank and Joe had their first chance for a close look at Simon.

He was about fourteen, but extremely tall for his age and wiry in build. He had dark, tangled hair that had not been cut for some time.

As Simon sat disconsolately, Frank examined a deep, ugly cut on the boy's leg. "No wonder he was limping. Get the first-aid kit, Joe."

Though Simon watched them all suspiciously, he seemed frightened rather than savage. Both Hardys were struck by the gentle look in the boy's face. When Joe returned with the first-aid kit he submitted meekly while his wound was washed and dressed. Joe applied a stinging antiseptic, but Simon barely winced with pain.

"Don't worry, Simon, you'll live," said Joe in a friendly voice as he straightened up. "And what a basketball player you'd make with your height!"

Bewildered, the boy continued to watch the Hardys closely, as though fearing some harm.

"Here we are, Simon," Chet Morgan called cheerily as he entered with the soup and sandwiches.

Simon ate greedily. Chet winked at Frank and Joe, then went to make more sandwiches and bring in some doughnuts. They were soon gone.

Chet grinned. "I'm glad to see that somebody besides me has a healthy appetite."

While Chet and Simon were finishing the food, Frank and Joe moved out to the kitchen.

In a low voice Joe said, "Simon doesn't look so fierce to me. I'm certain he's not the person we saw spying on us in the hollow yesterday. Simon's tall, and has long legs, but his face sure isn't the same one we saw."

Frank nodded agreement. "It was Donner who told us the person was probably Simon."

The boys were puzzled, but had no chance to talk further, as Chet and Simon came into the kitchen.

Chet began to play with Mystery. "Poor little pup," he said fondly. "Old Chet won't forget to feed you, too. No, sir. He'll do it right now."

He opened a can of puppy food, dumped it into a bowl, and set it on the floor. The little dog attacked it happily.

Simon, meanwhile, had put on his clothes, now dry from the heat of the stove. He watched Chet intently, then gave a shy, approving smile.

"Say," the stout boy muttered as he poked into a cupboard, "here's some dog food. Captain Maguire must have had a dog. Wonder if he went with him?"

Frank had noticed the mute boy's smile. "Simon likes the way Chet treats dogs," he thought. "Now's our chance to find out why he stole Mystery! But how can he answer us?" he asked himself, baffled. "He can't talk!"

Suddenly Frank had an idea. He went back to the living-room and returned with a pad of paper and a pencil which he placed on the kitchen table in front of the mute boy. Simon looked up questioningly, but without suspicion now.

"Simon," said Frank slowly and distinctly, "tell us—why did you run away with the dog?" At the same time he pointed to the beagle.

The boy's eyes looked puzzled for a minute. Then he seized the pencil and began to sketch.

Swiftly the picture of a tall, broad-shouldered man took shape. Simon darkened in heavy eyebrows and a moustache.

"It's Donner!" cried Joe in amazement.

"Wait!" Frank warned. "Simon hasn't finished."

As Frank, Joe and Chet crowded round, Simon rapidly drew the tall man's arm and hand in the act of grasping a little dog with Mystery's markings!

"He's telling us that Donner stole Mystery!" Joe cried out.

· 11 ·

The Tailor's Clue

"THERE's no doubt!" Joe exclaimed. "Simon's sketch tells us that Donner is the one who took Mystery!"

"Wait!" Frank commanded. "He's drawing something else!"

With a series of swift, sure stokes, the mute boy surrounded his drawing of Donner and the beagle with sketches of various dogs—a cocker spaniel, a German shepherd, and two hounds.

"What's this little one he's shading in with the pencil?" Joe asked. "A grey dog?"

"Grey or brown," Frank returned. "See, he's left one ear white."

"Brown with a white ear—that's Bobby Thompson's Skippy!" exclaimed Chet. "So Donner stole Skippy, too!"

Upon hearing the man's name, Simon raised his head once with an angry scowl, then finished his picture by drawing a line from each dog to Donner.

Then the mute boy stood up quickly from the table. His eager eyes showed that he had something more to communicate. He pointed to Donner's picture, then to Mystery. Suddenly Simon crouched down behind a chair and peered out.

"He's trying to tell us that he was hiding—behind a tree, perhaps," Frank interpreted.

Simon's one arm was tensed, with the fingers spread as though holding something heavy. "As if he's holding a rock or club," Frank deduced.

Abruptly Simon leaped out from behind the chair. He struggled with an imaginary antagonist, swinging the hand that held the "rock". Next, he seemed to clutch something else, in both arms and to be running away with it.

"That's Mystery he's holding now!" Chet said. excitedly. "He means he waited in ambush for Donner tonight, then hit him with a rock and ran off with Mystery himself!"

"Oh, great!" thought the bewildered Joe. "Simon and Donner are blaming the dog stealing on each other now. Who *is* guilty?"

While Frank and Chet, too, looked puzzled, Joe said aloud, "Well, there's one thing I want to know." He turned to Simon. "Why did you throw stones at us this afternoon?"

Going to the table once more, Simon quickly produced sketches of three very lifelike rattlesnakes. Frowning, he looked at Frank and Joe, and made as though to push them away with his hands.

"I get it! He was trying to warn us about those deadly snakes, not hurt us," Frank said.

"Well, he sure picked a forceful way to do it!" Joe rubbed his forehead ruefully. "That would mean he didn't think we were in cahoots with Donner."

Frank nodded. "Simon's given us something to work with. It seems pretty clear the self-styled hermit has been stealing dogs, and for my money, that ties him in with Captain Maguire's disappearance, too."

"You think the captain went after the dog thief

himself and then ran into trouble?" Joe queried.

"Well, apparently the captain had a dog," his brother reasoned. "Now suppose Donner stole the animal and Captain Maguire traced him to the hollow. Then suppose when he got down there the captain saw something he wasn't supposed to see."

"Then Donner, or somebody, had to get him out of the way because he knew too much!" Joe finished grimly. "Remember the blood we found on the leaves?"

Absorbed in this new possibility, Frank, Joe, and Chet failed to notice that Simon had been making his way quietly towards the back door. In a moment the tall boy had slipped out into the night!

"Hey!" called Chet. "Stop him!"

"No, let him go," said Frank Hardy calmly. "Simon's on our side, all right."

"I just wish we could do something to help him," Joe put in. "With his talent for drawing he might make out very well in spite of his handicap. He should go to a special art school."

Frank agreed, then said reflectively, "I can't seem to get Colonel Thunder out of my mind, and his resemblance to Donner. Also, I wonder if it could be more than coincidence that the German word for thunder is *donner*. What do you say we find the carnival, and talk to the colonel? He just *might* be a relative of of Donner."

"Suppose we drive to Forestburg in the morning," Joe suggested. "Maybe we can learn something there about the Donner family, and find out where the carnival is. Besides, it's about time we called Mother to see how things are in Bayport!"

Morning dawned bright and fresh after the rain, making everything seem greener than before, and the boys' spirits rose. Frank and Joe emerged from the cabin, followed by Chet, who cradled Mystery in his arms. But suddenly Frank stopped and frowned.

"Oh—oh! So much excitement last night we forgot to put up the convertible top before the storm. Now, look!"

Sure enough, there were puddles on the floor of the Hardys' car, and the seats, though protected by covers, were wet. The boys mopped up the water.

"Let's take Captain Maguire's car," said Joe. "If the captain's enemies see it, they may think he escaped, and that will bring them into the open."

The three set off with Joe at the wheel, Frank beside him, and Mystery and Chet in the rear.

Apparently the back seat was comfortable, for by the time the car entered Forestburg, both Chet Morton and the beagle were fast asleep.

"Let 'em alone." Frank laughed. "Last night was too exciting, I guess. You and I can do the detective work, Joe."

The two boys walked to the courthouse. Because it was only eight o'clock, the streets had little traffic. Frank and Joe, alert with curiosity, looked around. Many stores had offices above. In one upstairs window, which Joe pointed out, was a small sign:

WYKCOFF WEBBER
Attorney-at-Law

The brothers crossed the street to the courthouse. No one was at work yet.

"Well, let's try the shops," suggested Joe. "Somebody here must know the Donners."

During the next hour the two young detectives went from shop to shop asking questions about the Donner family. Although one or two shop assistants or store-keepers admitted the name "sounded familiar", nobody could give any definite information.

"I'll tell you what we're up against," said the exasperated Joe. "Some of these people are new in town, and they just don't know the Donners. The others know them, but won't talk to us. We're out-siders, and they think we're prying into local affairs that aren't any of our business!"

"Maybe so," agreed Frank. "But there's one shop I have to visit fast!" He indicated a tailor's establish-ment at the end of the street.

"What for?" demanded his brother, puzzled.

"Just discovered," muttered Frank, "I have a hole in my slacks—must have caught them on the rocks last night!"

A little man with shining bald head and thin black hair at the temples greeted them across the counter of the shop. "Yes?"

"Can you mend a pair of trousers while I wait?" Frank asked him.

The little man smiled, showed two gold teeth. "Of course. Will you come into the back shop, please?"

A moment later Frank and Joe were seated in the back room. Articles to be mended lay in a heap on the floor. Snippets of cloth were everywhere. Taking Frank's trousers, the man sat down at his work-table and examined the rip.

A roll of handsome, untouched suiting drew Frank's

attention. "Do you have many orders for tailor-made suits?" he asked the tailor curiously.

The little man sighed. "In this country, no," he answered. "Now it is all ready-made suits. There is no real work for a tailor any more, only patching holes, altering trousers.

"Forty years I've had this shop," the man went on reminiscently as he mended. "Now my main business is dry cleaning. But twenty, thirty years ago, we had people that liked fine clothes, tailored clothes! The Blackwells, Altgelts, Donners. Many fine suits I have made for them!"

"Donner?" repeated Frank.

"Yes, the Donners. A fine old family when I first came here. A family with style, distinction—they knew good clothes. There was old Mr Donner, a tall, handsome man. And his wife, oh, she was stylish. And a beautiful daughter there was, and twin boys—tall, good-looking fellows like the father. Looked so much alike you couldn't tell them apart."

"Twins!" Joe exclaimed. But instantly he suppressed his excitement, and asked casually, "Must have been quite a family. What became of them?"

The tailor shook his head. "Scattered. Old folks gone, of course. . . . The young lady? I don't know. Mr William, one of the twins—he's left town too. Only Mr Walter I see once in a while." The man sighed. "He doesn't dress up like he used to. Just wears sport clothes and doesn't come in here any more."

In high excitement, Frank put on his mended slacks. "By the way," he asked the tailor, "do you know where Klatch's Carnival is now? We've seen it once, but my brother here would like to see the show again."

Silently the man rummaged in a wastebasket, and then handed Frank an old poster with the carnival's schedule printed on it. Elated, the boys hurried from the shop. On their way to the car Frank stopped at an outdoor telephone kiosk to call his mother.

"Everything's well here, Frank," came Mrs Hardy's familiar musical voice from Bayport. "The latest word from Dad is that the men he's after are very clever, and he hasn't made much headway on the case."

Laughingly, his mother added, "Iola sends her love to her brother Chet."

"How about Joe?" asked Frank, grinning through the glass of the kiosk at his brother outside. Lively Iola Morton was Joe's girl-friend. "And, Mother, have you heard from Callie lately?" Callie Shaw was Frank's own favourite girl.

"Not a word. You boys had better not stay away too long, or both girls will find other escorts."

When Frank left the kiosk he found his brother staring across the street. Directly opposite the boys was a house with a doctor's sign.

"Look who's coming down the path!" Joe whispered. "Walter Donner!"

Frank's eyes followed the tall man, who evidently had not seen them. Donner wore a white bandage wrapped round his head.

"Guess Simon really did hit him with a rock," said Joe.

"Sure looks like it," Frank replied. "Come on! Let's see if we can find Klatch's Carnival for a talk with Donner's double. Colonel Bill Thunder may tell us something interesting!"

· 12 ·

Chet's Ruse

BACK at the old car Chet was still asleep, but Mystery greeted Frank and Joe with excited yapping.

"What . . . ? Who . . . ?" grunted the fat boy, starting up and blinking. "Are we still in Forestburg?"

While he sat rubbing his eyes, Frank and Joe, grinning, climbed into the front seat of the car.

"Are we in Forestburg?" repeated Joe with mock disgust. "We've only been here two hours, that's all. And listen to this!" He related what the brothers had learned.

Chet was astounded—and also disappointed not to have been there to hear his friends' discoveries first-hand. Meanwhile, Frank had been poring over a road map. Now he started the car and headed out of town in a westerly direction.

"Say!" Chet exclaimed. "Where are we off to now?"

"Riverville," Frank replied, and explained that Klatch's Carnival was there. "This side road should get us to the place in half the time the main road would take."

With an injured look on his broad face, the stout boy sat back and folded his arms. "So you walked out on me. You two just wait. I'll show you who's the detective round here!"

"We'll wait!" Joe chuckled.

Captain Maguire's old car seemed well suited to the narrow, badly rutted road. Manoeuvring carefully to avoid holes, Frank drove past dense woods that lined both sides. Sometimes the road followed a stream, at others it ran along ridges. There were no buildings in this area.

"We must be getting close," observed Frank, looking at the speedometer. "But what a place to run out of petrol!"

No sooner had the youth spoken than the three friends, rounding a turn, came upon a van parked on the left side of the road. The bonnet pointed skywards. Across each wing leaned a man in blue dungarees, his head almost invisible under the bonnet as both peered at the engine.

"Let's see what we can do," said Frank, pulling over. "We have plenty of time."

As the boys stepped from their car a huge dog bounded swiftly towards them.

"Oh, oh!" said Chet hastily. "Better stay inside, Mystery!" The big dog gave a curious but not un-friendly sniff at Frank's outstretched hand.

At the same moment one of the men straightened up. He was of thin build and had red hair. "Here, Blue!" he called and turned to greet the boys. "Don't you fellows worry about Blue. He won't bother nobody."

"What's the trouble?" Frank asked.

"She conked out, somehow," the man answered with a perplexed grin. "Just won't go!"

Joe was already peering at the engine. "Mind if we have a look? My brother and I have done a good bit of work on engines."

"Help yourself," invited the other man, who wore a loud printed shirt. "Got to do something—can't stay here all morning!"

Somewhat puzzled at the helplessness of the two men, Frank and Joe rolled up their sleeves.

"Got any tools?" Joe asked the man.

"Nope," the red-haired one answered. "Wouldn't you just know it?"

"Have much trouble with her?" Frank inquired.

The man scratched his head and grinned. "Well, now, I can't say, 'cause she's not mine. Just borrowed her, y'see, to deliver all these apples."

"Apples?" Chet beamed, and he strolled round to the back of the van, which was open. There, under a tarpaulin, were several bushel baskets of big red apples. "Mind if I try one, mister?"

"Go ahead," the thin man called.

Thinking that the second basket held juicier fruit than the one near the door, Chet chose his apple from there. But as he brought his hand away he noticed there was no fruit underneath—just something wrapped in brown paper!

Instantly a wave of suspicion flooded Chet's mind. What could the two men be hiding under their apples? The stout boy pondered a moment, remembering the hijacking near the state line.

Munching loudly, he strolled back towards the others. A sign, KENDRICK SCHOOL FOR BOYS, caught his eye on the van door. Continuing to munch idly, Chet managed to bump into Joe, who was bringing a spanner over from Captain Maguire's car.

"Oof—look where you're going!" he said loudly. In an undertone he added quickly, "Pretend you need a part and send me to town for the police."

Joe gave no sign, but went back to work. Still chewing, Chet strolled near.

"What's the situation here, fellows?" he complained. "I'm dying of starvation!"

Joe's calm voice replied from under the bonnet. "Well, pal, you'll just have to starve a little longer. We need a new condenser for this engine. How about running into town to get it?"

"Me!" Chet feigned indignation. "Why should I run the errands?"

"Okay, forget it. But you *could* get yourself some lunch in town."

As Chet ran towards the car, the red-haired man and his partner chuckled heartily. Fifteen minutes' fast, bumpy driving brought the stout boy back to Forestburg. Entering the familiar wooden courthouse, Chet made straight for Sheriff Ecker's office.

"Not you boys again," said the sheriff, who seemed even busier and more weary than before. "Look, son, I just don't have time for you now."

"You will when you hear this, Sheriff," was Chet's quick answer. "I think we've found a couple of your hijackers. Better come and look at them, anyway."

"What? Where?" The sheriff stood up so fast his swivel chair rolled rapidly backwards.

"Stalled about two miles out on the old Riverville Road. My buddies are keeping them there!"

While the amazed lawman listened, Chet told his suspicions. Even as he was speaking, the sheriff picked up his telephone. "Give me the headmaster at the Kendrick School for Boys!"

Shooting fast, direct questions, the sheriff got his

answers and relayed them to the waiting Chet.

"He says they never lend their van—it's the only one they have. . . . See if it's there now, will you?" he asked the headmaster.

In a few minutes he had his answer. "Gone! Stolen!" he told Chet, hanging up. "They just noticed it. Looks as if you're on to something, boy. Are they armed? Notice any weapons?"

Chet shook his head. "Nothing but a big dog that could be pretty mean if it wanted to."

After calling two regular deputies into his office, Sheriff Ecker explained his plan. "We'll wear our street clothes, boys. No badges. I'll take my personal car. We'll approach from the direction of Riverville. This boy here will be standing in the middle of the road, so we'll have to stop. Then we'll arrest those men."

Meanwhile, Frank and Joe had continued to tinker industriously at the engine of the van. The red-haired man and his helper seemed to grow less friendly as time passed. They continually looked up and down the road.

At last Captain Maguire's old car came into sight. Chet got out with a gleaming bunch of yellow bananas in one hand and a box containing a motor accessory part in the other.

"About time!" shouted Joe, who was feeling the tension.

Unconcernedly, Chet handed over the part, peeled himself a banana, and then planted himself in the middle of the road, munching, to watch the work go on. The two men watched now with worried faces.

"Of all the dunderheads!" Frank suddenly exclaimed in disgust. "This condenser isn't even for this make of car! Can't you ever think what you're doing? It's too small."

"No good?" demanded the men in chorus.

"We'll try to make it do," Frank grumbled.

Beep! Beep! Beep! A brown, weather-beaten saloon with three men seated together in the front, had approached quietly from the direction of Riverville and was now honking impatiently for Chet to get out of the road.

"Okay, hold your horses," he said. "I'll move."

Chet sauntered back to the stalled vehicle. But unnoticed by Frank, Joe, and the suspects, two men had stepped from the saloon and come over. With drawn pistols, the deputies moved into position behind the red-haired man and his partner.

"Raise your hands!" ordered one quietly. "Turn round and don't try anything. You're under arrest!"

Caught completely off guard, the men did as they were told. Meanwhile the third man, Sheriff Ecker, who carried a large net under one arm, went swiftly to the back of the stolen van. He ripped off the tarpaulin and, heaving out apples, shouted:

"Furs! You were right, son. Look at these!"

The excited sheriff carried an armload of rich, expensive furs.

Frank and Joe, with greasy hands and faces, merely stared from Chet to the sheriff to the captives in amazement.

"You'd better talk," Ecker warned the men as he checked a notebook. "These furs were stolen three months ago from a trailer in Jersey. You've been hiding them until you thought the 'heat' was off. They're concrete evidence against you!"

For answer, the thin man suddenly uttered a sharp command. "Blue! At 'em, boy!"

At once the huge hound bared its teeth and advanced ferociously upon the two officers. But at that moment the sheriff raced up and hurled the big net over the raging animal. In a moment, with the Hardys' help, the dog was helpless.

"Why, you fat . . ." began the red-haired man in a rage.

Chet Morton, however, merely looked at Frank and Joe with a satisfied grin on his face.

"All right, fellows, who's the detective now?" he demanded.

After handcuffing the prisoners securely, the officers led them to the sheriff's car.

"Nice work, boys," Ecker said. "I'll get back to town. Have to report the recovery of these furs *and* the capture of these men to the FBI?"

The sheriff and one of the officers put the prisoners in their car, while the third officer drove the van. The boys said good-bye and continued on towards Riverville.

"You get all the credit this time, Chet," Joe praised his friend. "You're getting places as a detective!"

On the outskirts of town Frank stopped at a telephone kiosk and called Fenton Hardy at a State Police Headquarters just over the New Jersey border. He told of Captain Maguire's disappearance and the hijackers' capture, then continued:

"No news of Captain Maguire yet, Dad, but we're following a new lead right now."

"Good work," he said. "And give Chet my congratulations."

The boys started up once more. "The carnival's on the far edge of town," said Frank.

"Not so fast," Chet spoke up. "Lunch first. Who's the detective round here, anyhow?"

"Okay." It was more than an hour before Frank, Joe, and Chet entered Klatch's Carnival for the third time. A friendly ticket collector directed them to a small, blue caravan trailer parked behind the tents where Colonel Thunder performed his act.

Frank knocked. As the man looked at them inquiringly, Frank put the question:

"Pardon me, sir, but aren't you William Donner?"

· 13 ·

Worrisome Watching

STARTLED, the animal trainer fidgeted uneasily with the door handle.

"What gave you the idea I'm William Donner?" he asked.

Frank, seeing the man's embarrassment, chose his words carefully.

"Well, we've met a man named Walter Donner, who looks exactly like you. When we found out that he had an identical twin brother, we put two and two together. And then, the names 'William Donner' and 'Bill Thunder' are the same—*donner* being the word for thunder in German."

In spite of himself, the man gave an approving smile at this last deduction.

"All right, boys," he said as he faced them once more. "I'm William Donner, and I don't suppose it matters if anybody knows it. You see, we Donners used to be a fine, close-knit family. But when my parents died, my brother and sister and I couldn't agree on dividing the estate. So far as I know, the properties are still vacant, and the lawyers are still arguing.

"I had to make a living, so I took this job. I've always been able to train animals. I didn't want to embarrass my brother and sister—they were always

98

touchy about their social position—so I just translated the family name to Thunder."

Pausing for a moment, the tall man seemed to reflect. "So you saw Walter! I didn't even realize he was still in this part of the country. Haven't heard from him in years. What's he doing with himself now?"

"Not much," Frank answered. "He lives in a little cabin down in Black Hollow, and raises a few sheep."

At this, the colonel raised his prominent eyebrows in disbelief. "Walter? Living in that old shack? Why, that's impossible. Walter always loved luxury—couldn't do without it."

"He seems pretty comfortable, Mr Donner," Chet put in.

"Maybe." Colonel Thunder went on. "But you don't understand what a come down this is for my brother! I'm sorry to hear it. He's raising sheep, you say?"

"Yes," Frank answered. "In fact, we saw him buying one at the auction. We thought it was you."

The colonel nodded, still reflecting on the strange news. "Funny both of us should be making a living, even a poor one, from animals," he mused. "You see, we all loved animals. Walter was different, though. He could be cruel to them, too—couldn't stand it when they disobeyed him."

"Cruel to them?" Joe Hardy picked up the words. "Would it surprise you to know, Mr Donner, that your brother is suspected of kidnapping dogs?"

The man who called himself Colonel Thunder looked at the boys in the commanding way that seemed to be a trait of the Donner family. "Yes, it would!" he snapped, as though he himself had been insulted.

"Not only that," Frank continued with determination. "We have reason to believe that your brother is involved in the disappearance of a friend of ours, Captain Thomas Maguire."

"See here! What are you trying to pull on me?" Colonel Thunder demanded indignantly. "My twin has some strange ideas, but he wouldn't harm anybody. What are you prying round here for, anyway? Get out! And take your ridiculous accusations with you!"

With that, he closed the blue metal door of the trailer in their faces. Frank, Joe, and Chet were obliged to turn away.

"Boy, was he angry!" said Chet as the three walked to their car. "Do you suppose he's in cahoots with his brother?"

Frank shook his head thoughtfully. "No. He was genuinely shocked at our story, that's all. Colonel Thunder still seems to be touchy about his family's honour. Say, maybe our news will make him pay a call on his long-lost brother!"

"Yes, and maybe warn him of our suspicions," added Joe. "I suggest we sneak down into the hollow tonight and see what goes on."

"Good idea," Frank approved.

"Well, if it's all the same to you," put in Chet, "Mystery and old Chet will stay up in the cabin. I've had enough of these woods by night. Besides, after this morning's bit of detective work, I think I may say I've earned a rest."

"You have," Frank agreed, and Joe laughed. "Will we never hear the end of it?"

The three drove back to Forestburg. They stopped

at the courthouse and learned from Sheriff Ecker that the prisoners had been sent under heavy guard to New Jersey, where Mr Fenton Hardy, one of the chief investigators in the hijacking case, would question them.

"Is that a fact?" Frank asked mildly, giving Joe a wink.

"Yes, sir," Sheriff Ecker declared emphatically. "He's a real famous detective they called in on it. You boys ever hear of him?"

"Now and then." Joe grinned.

"Say, what are you two grinning about?" The Sheriff frowned. "Hardy. Isn't that your last name, Frank and Joe? No relation, by chance?"

"Distant relation," Joe answered with a straight face. "About a hundred miles distant right now, I believe. He's our father."

"Well, I'll be . . ." Words failed the stocky, good-natured sheriff for a moment. Then his face became serious again. "And what about your friend, boys? Hasn't come back yet, has he?"

Joe, about to pour out their suspicions of Walter Donner, was stopped by a nudge from Frank. "No, Sheriff," Frank replied, "but we're working on it. We'll let you know if anything turns up."

After one final stop in Forestburg at Giller's General Store for more groceries, Frank, Joe, and Chet at last climbed into the captain's old car for the trip back to Black Hollow.

"Why not tell the sheriff about Donner being a dog thief?" Joe asked as he drove.

"Because we still have to prove ourselves to Sheriff Ecker," Frank answered grimly. "Walter Donner made us look pretty incompetent in front of the sheriff. Any accusation we bring against him is going to need plenty of proof—no matter who our father is. Wait till we've really got the goods on Donner. Then we'll show the sheriff!"

To prepare for their long vigil that evening, the brothers lay down for a nap as soon as they reached Captain Maguire's cabin. At sundown they were awakened by Chet Morton, who had prepared an appetizing dinner.

"About time for the night shift," he called. "Don't forget to put on dark clothing."

Soon a clear, cloudless sky, in which the stars sparkled brightly, spread itself over Black Hollow.

"The moon isn't due to rise until very late," Frank noted as the brothers prepared for their expedition. "That gives us an advantage since we're doing the spying."

A moment later, alert and refreshed by their sleep and fortified by Chet's meal, Frank and Joe slipped out from the back door of the little cabin. As soon as their eyes became accustomed to the darkness, they entered the woods.

By now the path into the mysterious hollow was familiar to them even at night. They moved along the trail noiselessly but swiftly, without using torches.

Frank noted that it was the first time he had not had the eerie feeling of being followed in the woods.

"I suppose it's because we're in a position to do the following ourselves," he thought with a smile.

The boys avoided the exposed parts of the trail entirely, moving amongst the densely-growing trees instead. At length they reached the little clearing where Donner's strange cabin stood. In the complete darkness they could see nothing but an indistinct mass of rocks and logs in front of them. The little building was invisible, except for a thin orange line of light round the frame of the closed door.

Cautiously Frank led the way as close as possible to the door without exposing themselves to the view of anyone else who might be in the surrounding woods.

They found a suitable place and stopped to listen. The sound of voices came to them plainly from inside the cabin—Walter Donner's voice, somewhat subdued, and the thin, whining voice of Wyckoff Webber, the attorney! The Hardys were astounded.

"I tell you, I've been to see Elizabeth," Webber was saying, "and she won't budge an inch."

There was a sound as of somebody moving a chair impatiently.

"Well"—Donner's big voice rumbled—"I'm fed up with this life. Fed up with it. I want my share of the estate!"

"You don't think I'm fed up with it?" the lawyer replied irritably. "I want my money, too. Well, let's get down to business. How are things going?"

When they heard this question, Frank and Joe waited breathlessly for an answer. But none came. There was a further scraping of furniture. That was all.

"Didn't Donner reply?" Frank wondered. "Or is he showing Webber something?"

While the young sleuth pondered, crouching in the dark, the sudden pressure of his brother's hand roused his attention. Now Frank heard the sound of stealthy footsteps approaching through the woods along the path!

From their hiding-place Frank and Joe could easily watch the break in the woods where the path entered the clearing. But though they waited soundlessly, no figure appeared. A chill of suspense ran down the brothers' spines.

"Is it Colonel Thunder?" Joe asked himself. "Or Simon?" Meanwhile, no further sound came from within the house, either.

For about fifteen minutes the silence continued. The unknown intruder was no longer moving, but the boys wondered, was he lurking in the darkness a few scant yards from the Hardys themselves?

"Somebody has trailed us down here," Joe thought uneasily, "and he's waiting for us to make the first move!"

· 14 ·

Flash Fire

WITHOUT changing his position, Joe moved enough so he could whisper to his brother.

"Somebody's watching us," he murmured. "Waiting for us to show ourselves!"

Frank, after considering a moment, placed his own lips close to Joe's ear and replied:

"Check! We'll outwait him."

Straining their eyes vainly against the darkness, Frank and Joe examined the break in the woods which marked the exit from the path. All they could make out, however, was the dark clump of bushes where the intruder must be hidden. Whoever he was, he was keeping just as still and silent as they were!

Abruptly, the loud voices of Donner and Webber in the cabin could be heard once more. Their remarks were no longer muffled.

"We'll get some money pretty soon," Donner's voice rumbled. "I'm desperate enough to take a chance."

After a pause, Webber's irritable tones were heard in reply, "I'll attend to the boys. Nothing can go wrong this time!"

Hearing these words, Frank frowned to himself, puzzled. Were he and Joe and Chet "the boys" that the two were talking about? Before the youth could make up his mind, there was a rusty squeaking sound, and the door of the cabin was thrown open.

For an instant the lawyer's small plump figure and Donner's tall, commanding one were outlined against the light of the two oil-lamps within. Then the door was closed and the lawyer crossed the clearing. He made no attempt to soften his footsteps.

Frank's keen eyes suddenly spotted an abrupt, blurred movement in the dark bushes at the entrance to the trail. Whoever was there was hiding from Webber as well as from them.

In another moment the lawyer had entered the woods. His footsteps quickly receded in the darkness. Still warily watching the bushes, Frank and Joe saw a man step out. For a moment he stood still, a dark form barely silhouetted against the faint glow of the starlight. Then soundlessly he entered the woods on the trail of the retreating Webber.

"He was spying on Webber!" Joe whispered. "Shall we tail the two of them and see what happens?"

"No," Frank decided quickly. "Let's stick to our plan of staying here and waiting for Colonel Thunder to show up."

Slowly, silently, the night wore on. The constellations changed their positions in the sky. In the east a pale glow appeared. At last a crescent moon showed itself above the trees. A light but chilly breeze sprang up.

Although the night was clear, the heavy early-morning dew of the mountains now covered everything. The boys' clothing, in particular their shoes and the legs of their jeans, was drenched from the long walk. Now the rest of their clothing felt damp and the cold breeze chilled them. Their legs were cramped from the long wait. They could see their breaths in the pale light thrown by the new moon.

No one else came to visit Walter Donner. At last the crack of light outlining the door of the little cabin could be seen no longer.

"I guess he's gone to bed," Frank whispered to Joe. "We may as well go back to the cabin and hit the hay ourselves."

Using the same caution which they had practised on the trek down, the two boys made their way through the dark woods to Captain Maguire's cabin. As they were climbing the steep, familiar path out of the hollow, Frank suddenly laid a hand on Joe's arm.

"Listen!" he whispered.

From the depths of Black Hollow came an eerie sound, at first soft, then louder. It was a long, plaintive wail.

"Screech owl," Joe noted. "Where's it coming from?"

"Other end of the hollow," Frank answered after listening carefully. "In fact, I'd say somewhere pretty close to Donner's place."

"Hmmm! Funny nobody startled an owl earlier, with all that coming and going down there tonight," observed Joe.

"I'm glad we didn't meet one," Frank said. "They have a quiet, spooky flight that makes people take them for ghosts."

In another minute the brothers had reached the rim of the valley. Lights burned cheerfully in the windows of Captain Maguire's cabin.

"Boy! Am I glad to see you two!" exclaimed Chet,

jumping up from the bunk as they entered. "That witch, or owl, is on the loose again. It woke me up. You heard it?"

"We sure did," Frank replied.

"Brr!" Joe shivered. "Never mind the owl. Just let me near that stove."

"If that's the way you feel," said Chet, "I'll whip up a little snack. I could use something hot, myself."

A little later, over mugs of hot chocolate, the Hardys told Chet of their vigil outside the windowless cabin.

"So," Joe concluded, "Webber is Donner's lawyer, apparently, and they both want money."

"Birds of a feather flock together," Chet observed, adding with a grimace, "but I don't like the sound of Webber's threat to 'attend to the boys.' "

"This Webber is always croaking about money," Joe remarked. "What money do you think he means?"

"They must've been talking about the Donner estate tonight," Frank put in. "Remember, Colonel Thunder told us the lawyers were still arguing about it? And Donner said he was tired of waiting—that he was getting desperate."

"Too bad Colonel Thunder didn't show up," said Joe. "After all, part of that money is his."

"Well, there doesn't seem to be anything dishonest going on," Chet pointed out. "Donner was only talking about money he has a claim to. And another thing—Webber told us Captain Maguire owed him money. Do you suppose the captain never went into the hollow at all, but just ran away somewhere?"

Frank shook his head decisively. "You don't know Captain Maguire, Chet. He never ran away from anything in his life, much less a debt to a character like Webber!"

"You know what I wonder?" Joe said suddenly. "Donner says he's getting desperate, I wonder what he'll *do?*"

"What a puzzle!" exclaimed Chet, shaking his head. "We'll never figure it out tonight, fellows. Let's just forget it for a while, and make a fresh start in the morning!"

Frank and Joe needed no further urging. After changing to dry underclothes, the two boys unrolled their sleeping bags and climbed in.

"Four o'clock," noted Chet as he turned out the lamps and climbed into bed. "Only a few hours of sleep till breakfast. Let's use them."

"All the same, I'd like to know who was hiding in those bushes," came Joe's drowsy mumble in the dark room. In another moment all was silent.

As he lay in his sleeping bag, Frank was still wondering about the mysterious person who had been hiding near them. In the boy's tired brain, all the perplexing questions of the strange case seemed to whirl madly round and round.

Who had been lurking near Donner's cabin? Where was Captain Maguire?

When Frank dozed off, he had peculiar, fitful dreams. First, he saw a pack of barking dogs being chased by a witch on a broomstick. Next, the dogs turned into owls, which flew round hooting and wailing.

Meanwhile, the witch had turned into Walter Donner, who seemed to be talking calmly to some sheep. Then, weirdly, Walter became William Donner

—Colonel Thunder—and the sheep became a snarling black puma.

Colonel Thunder's huge black whip cracked again and again. "Oh-h!" Frank moaned aloud.

Now, in his dream, he heard Wyckoff Webber's rasping voice, "I'll attend to the boys. Nothing can go wrong this time!"

Once more, Frank seemed to see the little lawyer standing in the open doorway of Walter Donner's cabin, talking with Donner. Behind them the orange-yellow flames of the oil-lamp were burning—burning—

Burning! It seemed to Frank as if he could even smell the distinctive odour of burning oil, that he could feel the heat generated by the lamps! The yellow flames seemed to grow brighter and brighter in his dream until they blotted out everything else.

Again Colonel Thunder's black whip cracked. Suddenly Frank sat up, wide awake. He was facing the kitchen. For an instant the youth thought that someone had turned on the lights in there. Then, with horror, he realized that one whole side of the cabin was a mass of swirling yellow flame! The snapping and cracking was the sound of the timbers as they caught fire, as in some gigantic fireplace. The whole cabin had become an inferno!

"Joe! Chet!" he shouted frantically above the roar of the swirling flames. Frank pulled off his sleeping bag and wound it round him, as he shook his brother into consciousness. Then he leaped to the sleeping Chet.

"Joe! Wrap your sleeping bag round you and make a dash for the front door!" Frank screamed. By now all four walls were ablaze, and the heat was unbearable.

The three boys raced outside

Instantly taking in the situation, Joe followed instructions. Meanwhile, Frank helped put Captain Maguire's blankets round the still-groggy Chet, and now the three raced outside. Mystery, too, dashed to safety, yapping in fear.

The boys' hair and brows were singed, and their eyes smarted. The three friends watched in speechless dismay as the flames of the burning cabin lighted up the whole area like a beacon. Sparks shot a hundred feet skyward.

"Boy!" breathed Chet. "There goes all our stuff, and Captain Maguire's too—clothes, food, money, everything. But we're fortunate to get out alive! What woke you, Frank?"

"A lucky dream," Frank answered gratefully. "Luck was sure on our side."

Fortunately, the Hardys' convertible and Captain Maguire's car had been parked far enough away from the fire to be out of danger. But the cabin, with its drums of paraffin and petrol, burned fiercely out of control.

"No use driving anywhere to get help," said Frank. "No equipment could get here in time."

The trio, huddled in blankets and sleeping bags, stared at the flaming cabin.

"The walls seemed to go up all at once," Frank remarked to the others. "It wasn't as if the fire had started in the kitchen and spread to the living-room. Everything went up at once."

Joe looked grim. "No fire could start that way—unless—unless it was set deliberately by someone!"

· 15 ·

Ragged Footprints

CHET gulped. "The cabin was set on fire?" he cried.

"Right," said Joe.

Frank nodded. "From the way the fire spread, I'd say someone poured paraffin all around the foundation and then lit a match to it. I smelt paraffin strongly right at the beginning!"

Suddenly Frank and Joe recalled Webber's words: "I'll attend to the boys." Could it be that he was the incendiary?

"But that would make him a murderer!" Chet exclaimed. "Is he that bad?"

"Oh, we're not accusing him yet," Joe said quickly.

"Or anyone else," Frank added. "When it's safe to look in the ruins, we'll hunt for clues."

Helplessly, Frank, Joe, and Chet watched the blaze. Though the mysterious fire had begun suddenly, it burned for some time. The logs of the cabin, soaked in creosote to withstand the weather, now burned fiercely until consumed. When morning came, the once trim cabin was a mass of rubble, glowing here and there with orange sparks.

"It's a crime!" Joe said. "If somebody did burn down the cabin, I'd like to get my hands on him!"

Suddenly Chet pointed out, "Fellows, we haven't

a stitch of clothing except our underwear!"

Despite the gravity of the situation, all three boys began to laugh. "This is a fine situation," said Frank.

"Of course we have blankets and sleeping bags," Joe spoke up. "We can play Indian."

"But there's no food," Chet reminded him, "to have a feast."

"It seems funny that no one has come here to see where the fire is," Frank remarked. "You'd think a forest-fire observer would have spotted it from his tower and investigated."

No one arrived, however. When the intense heat had abated, Frank went towards the ruins. He noted that Captain Maguire had built his cabin on a stone foundation, using concrete for mortar. After finishing, he had spread his surplus gravel round the entire foundation.

Now the three young detectives found that this gravel still preserved the warmth of the fire. But even more important, it had preserved something else— several deep, distinct, footprints!

"You were right, Frank, about somebody starting this fire!" Joe exclaimed. "The prints are on all sides. If only we'd brought our moulding equipment from home, we could have made some fine plaster casts for evidence."

"We'll have to do without," replied his brother. "But we can still take measurements."

He placed his own bare right foot over the right indentation left by the suspect. "Somebody with a short, wide shoe," Frank observed. "And look here! All the left prints have this ragged outer edge. Looks as if the sole of the man's shoe had been damaged by a stone or a knife!"

So absorbed were Frank, Joe and Chet in examining the fresh prints that they were suddenly startled to discover someone standing directly behind them. Simon, the mute boy, had just appeared from the encircling woods. He gaped in astonishment at the blackened ruins.

"Hello, Simon," Joe called. Instantly he dropped his eyes from the boy's face to his feet. Frank and Chet, having the same idea, also looked down.

In spite of his long legs, Simon had average-size feet. And his battered tennis shoes could not have made the footprints in the gravel.

"Somebody burned us out, Simon," explained Joe. "Take a look at these prints!"

Though Simon followed Joe's pointing finger obediently, he merely shook his head and shrugged.

"Well, what do we do now?" Chet asked.

"First, let's get some clothes," Frank answered.

"Oh, sure," said Chet. "And what are we using for money and clothes to go into a shop with? Every cent we had was burned in the fire. We can't go shopping in our underwear!"

Mysteriously, Frank's face brightened. "Simon," he said, "you'll have to do our shopping for us." Frank quickly explained their needs to the mute boy. Simon nodded comprehension and consent.

"Now, the money." Taking a small screwdriver from the glove compartment of the car, Frank prised up the horn button. As the piece popped out, a note, folded very small, fell out too.

"Emergency money," explained Frank, grinning.

"Thank goodness," said Chet.

Once more the yellow convertible made its way over the hilly country roads to the town of Forestburg. Purposely, Frank parked the car a good hundred yards from the first house of the town.

"Nothing like driving in bare feet," he remarked. "Tickles!"

"What a sight we must be!" Joe laughed. "No clothes, singed eyebrows—refugees from a circus, or something!"

"At least Mystery still has his coat on," Chet joked.

"Quiet!" commanded Joe, and grinned. "I'm writing down sizes for the shop assistant. Let's see— trousers about six feet round the waist, Chet?"

Finally the lithe figure of Simon emerged from the car. He made his way, with some hesitation, down the street towards Giller's General Store.

As soon as he had gone, the three boys began to talk over the footprints around the burned cabin.

"I'll bet anything they belong to Webber," Joe declared.

Frank's suspicions were nearly as strong as Joe's, but he advised caution.

"Better hold your horses a little, Joe. This is a very serious charge. We'll need airtight proof before we can accuse Webber."

"And even if you're right," Chet spoke up, "why did Webber and Donner want us out of the way? What *is* it that he didn't want to go wrong?"

"Wish I knew," said Joe. "Since we're not involved in the estate, I'd say Webber and Donner must be tied up in some kind of underhand business. Maybe

Colonel Thunder is in it too, and got word to his brother about our visit to him."

"What a mess!" Chet said with a sigh. "Say," he added, looking at his watch. "Simon's been gone twenty minutes. What's he *doing* all this time! Suppose somebody should come by?"

"Duck, fellows! Here comes a lady!" Joe warned.

"Where? Is she close?" Chet and Frank scrambled to the floor.

"Guess I made a mistake!" Joe chuckled.

"Why, you joker," Frank theatened.

"Hey!" Chet moaned. "Maybe Simon has just run off with our money, and won't bring us any clothes!"

This remark made all the boys glum. But at last Simon's tall form could be seen approaching from the town. In his arms the mute boy carried a huge package wrapped in brown paper.

Eager hands reached from the car to snatch the package and change from the astonished Simon. Flying fingers ripped open the paper and tugged at the clothing inside.

"Keep watch, Simon. Warn us if anybody comes," ordered Joe.

In a few minutes three fully-clothed boys joined Simon on the pavement. All wore identical blue jeans, red cotton shirts, check socks, and sneakers.

"Jumpin' goldfish!" complained Chet. "We look like a comedy team on television!"

Simon grinned and from under his right arm produced a package containing three extra shirts. He threw them into the back seat, as the boys looked relieved.

While Frank and Joe merely laughed at each other's

singed hair and eyebrows, Chet said, "Breakfast before anything else!"

Customers in Forestburg's largest café peered in amusement over their morning coffee as the door opened. First came three boys, all wearing red shirts and blue jeans, with their hair and eyebrows partly singed away. Then came a tall, gangling boy with trousers too short and a wild shock of hair. Disregarding the curious stares, the four were soon putting away vast quantities of bacon rolls.

"Must be some of them carnival fellas," muttered one man to his neighbour. "Looks like somebody ran a blowlamp over those three!"

But Frank, Joe, Chet, and Simon ate heartily, still ignoring the customers' stares. While Simon and Chet worked on their third bacon roll each, the Hardys consulted briefly in whispers.

"Think we ought to reach Dad?" Joe asked his brother, "and tell him our suspicions about the fire?"

Frank, after a moment's reflection, decided against this. "Dad has enough on his hands, and he'd probably drop everything and come rushing over. Let's wait till we have proof to give him."

Joe then proposed, "How about seeing Webber before we try Elizabeth Donner?"

"Right," Frank approved. "But we'd better report to Sheriff Ecker first."

The face of the lawman became grave as he heard of the boys' narrow escape. He agreed to keep the matter quiet until the culprit's identity could be established beyond a doubt.

"Something funny's going on out at Black Hollow, all right," he admitted at last. "I'll send some men out there right away. We'll look over the wreckage and take casts of the footprints. I've sort of neglected you fellows, but this is serious business. I'll drop everything and get on to it. Where are you headed now?"

Frank gave his brother a quick warning look.

"We have to pick up a few things. That fire cleaned us out."

Sheriff Ecker and two members of his force started off to Black Hollow to investigate the fire. They took Simon and Mystery with them.

"I've arranged for Simon to take care of Mystery until we get back," Chet announced when the three were back in the car again. "Especially since we don't know where we'll be sleeping tonight!"

The boys then made straight for the building in which they had seen Wyckoff Webber's office. Frank parked and the three companions climbed the office building stairs. A small grey-haired woman, with a sharp nose, answered their knock.

"Are you Mr Webber's secretary?" Joe asked her.

"Secretary indeed! *Him* with a secretary. He's too miserly," the woman snorted. "I just post his letters. I can tell you he's out of town for a few days, if that's what you want to know!"

"Thank you," said Frank, and the boys trudged down the steps to the street.

"Now let's try to find Elizabeth Donner," declared Frank, leading the way back to the courthouse.

As he had hoped, the courthouse had a stack of telephone books for the towns some distance around.

"Everybody take a book," he directed. "Look up Miss Elizabeth Donner."

Less than ten minutes of silent work brought a sharp

exclamation from Joe. "Here she is—Miss Elizabeth Donner, with an address in Brookwood!"

The boys made sure there were no other women with the same name, then went to their car. After consulting a road map, the three chums set out for Brookwood, where they hoped to find out more about the strange Donner brothers!

· 16 ·

The First Find

SHORTLY before noon the yellow convertible rolled along the quiet main street of Brookwood. Large, pleasant white houses with wide lawns and lovely trees stood on either side.

"A nice old town," Frank commented, then added, "Fellows, let's be careful with Miss Donner, and not make the same mistake we did with Colonel Thunder."

"How do you mean?" queried Chet.

"We insulted his family pride. These Donners are touchy people. If we aren't careful of what we say, we won't learn anything."

"True," Joe agreed, "and maybe we can find out a little about Elizabeth from somebody here in town before we call on her. Then we can say we met her attractive brother while searching the woods for a man believed lost."

"Attractive!" snorted Chet.

"Okay, Chet," said Frank. "I'd like to know what this town thinks of Elizabeth, too. And here's the place to learn something."

Before Joe and Chet could protest, Frank had pulled up before one of the old town houses which had been converted into a business establishment.

" 'Blue Willow Tearoom'," Chet read from a sign

outside. "Oh, no! We're not eating in a tearoom. They wouldn't serve hot dogs, and that's what I want. Most of their customers are probably fussy old ladies on diets."

"Right you are." Frank chuckled. "And who should know more about Miss Donner than the old ladies? Anyway, I remember Mother mentioning that she once ate in this town. Let's go!"

A little bell tinkled discreetly as the door opened. Frank, Joe, and Chet, their singed hair combed as well as possible, and their red shirts buttoned at the collar, sat down awkwardly on dainty chairs placed round a little table.

"Good morning!" A tall woman of middle age, wearing a tiny starched apron, came forward and eyed them with sharp suspicion.

"Good morning," Frank responded with a wide smile. Rising to his feet, he said, "I think my mother stopped here at one time. We'd like to have some luncheon. How cool and restful a nice tearoom is on a hot day!"

Charmed by Frank's manner, the woman smiled. "What would you like, boys?"

To Chet's astonishment, he was soon enjoying a puffy omelette, tasty vegetable salad, and a tall glass of iced tea spiced with a sprig of mint fresh from the garden.

"Say," he declared, "I'll have to eat in tearooms more often!"

"Well, pick up your napkin," teased Joe. "That's the fifth time you've dropped it on the floor."

"This *is* Brookwood, isn't it?" Frank asked the woman when she brought strawberry gateau for dessert. Miss Elizabeth Donner lives here, doesn't she?"

"Oh, yes," the woman answered. "Perhaps your mother has ordered dresses from Miss Donner. She's a wonderful dress designer, you know. Customers come to her from all over. She works right in her own home."

"No," said Frank. "It wasn't that. We know some other members of her family."

"Oh, yes, Miss Donner comes from a very good old family. She's a lady, to be sure—but very firm, too, about her business. It's marvellous how well she does! The family has broken up though, I understand. I don't believe she ever sees her brothers now."

The woman went off to seat a new group of customers and the boys had no further chance to speak to her. A short while later, as the three friends walked towards Elizabeth Donner's house, Joe exclaimed, "A dress designer! What are we going to say to her, for Pete's sake?"

"We'll think of something," Frank replied confidently.

"You mean *you'll* think of something," Joe corrected him. "Count me out!"

"Me too," Chet chimed in.

With that, the two marched away, leaving Frank Hardy alone on the steps of a well-cared-for white-painted house. Near the door a little sign invited: *Ring Bell and Walk In.*

Frank found himself in a well-furnished sitting-room used as a waiting-room. Since no one was there, he had time to examine the thick rug, the fine furniture, the tasteful wall decorations, and the well-filled engagement book which stood open on a little table. Evidently Elizabeth Donner's business was a profitable one.

A door opened softly, and a tall, handsome woman in her late thirties, with dark hair and the commanding Donner look, came in. At the same time, a little brown dog scurried through the door at her feet and threw itself happily upon Frank.

Stooping to pat the animal, the youth noticed one white ear. His mind raced. A brown mongrel with one white ear! And no collar or name tag. Could this be Bobby Thompson's dog, Skippy?

Concealing his suspicions, Frank laughed and stood up. "Friendly little pup. Friend of mine had one just like him—maybe it's from the same litter. Where'd you get this dog, Miss Donner?"

"I really don't know where he came from." The woman's manner was friendly but firm. "A brother gave him to me. The poor little thing was lost and he befriended it, but couldn't keep it himself."

"Oh, was that the pleasant Mr Donner who went with me into Black Hollow to look for a lost friend of my family?"

Elizabeth Donner shot a searching look at her youthful visitor.

"I wouldn't know," she answered evenly. "By the way, what brought you here?"

Carefully Frank side-stepped the question. Hoping his voice sounded casual, he said, "I was wondering do you take clients living at a distance? My mother loves to wear attractive suits and dresses. Since I was in the neighbourhood I thought I'd ask you."

Miss Donner smiled. "You're an unusual boy, aren't you?" she said. "Not many sons are that thoughtful. Have your mother write to me. Then we'll see."

Watching the tall, self-possessed woman narrowly,

Frank wondered, "Is she playing a game? Does she believe me or doesn't she?" But Elizabeth Donner's smile told him nothing.

"I'll do that," he answered, and quickly left the house. Deep in thought, he returned to the car. He told the others what had transpired, adding, "I think I found Bobby Thompson's dog! Donner probably gave the pup to his sister soon after he stole it."

"Skippy?" Chet sat up, astonished. "What does that man do—steal dogs for the pleasure of giving them away?"

"Don't ask me," Frank answered. "That's all I could learn. Except that Miss Donner does very well with her dressmaking. I'd say she doesn't need any estate money—or any dishonest money, either. But you never know."

"Okay, so this is a blind alley," said the disgruntled Chet. "Where are we cooking and sleeping tonight?"

"There's only one place to solve the mystery of Black Hollow, and that's Black Hollow!" declared Joe. "I vote we camp near there."

Frank jingled the coins in his pocket. "We'd better solve it pretty soon," he warned. "Money's getting scarce. What will we need for tonight?"

"Some food," answered Chet, "and a couple of torches."

"And a pad and pencil, so Simon can communicate with us," put in Joe.

After buying these necessities, the three friends started back for Black Hollow. At Joe's suggestion, they drove slowly. "Let's take our time," he said, "and not get there until after dark. Then nobody will know we're around."

Accordingly, Chet prepared supper for them and at eight o'clock they headed once more for the hollow. Showing only parking lights, the big car climbed slowly up Rim Road. When they passed the lighted Thompson house, the boys knew they had nearly reached the top. Once there, the trio hid the car amongst some trees and started off on foot.

Only a few stars sparkled in the sky. Clouds, black as coal, were massing in the west. With a torch beam jabbing ahead into the darkness, Joe led Chet and Frank a little way along the hollow trail, and then off to one side.

"This spot's level and well sheltered," the youth explained. "I've had it in mind, in case we had to sleep out."

After unrolling their sleeping bags—Chet's had been in the car boot—the three boys removed their shoes and crawled in. Lying on their backs in the darkness, Frank and Joe stared upward at the trees. A light wind moved the branches and presently from the hollow came the sad, familiar wailing.

"Screech owl," Joe murmured.

A few minutes later the night was broken by a number of screams.

"Oh, oh, there's the witch again!" said Joe.

"Joe, that isn't the same screaming we heard on our first night here," Frank noted. "It's not so harsh, so insistent. This really sounds like a barn owl. The screaming the other night, I'm sure, was human!"

"Maybe." Joe yawned. "Anyhow, this one's an owl. Nothing to get excited about." In another moment Joe was asleep, then Frank.

"Help! Leave me alone!"

The cries came from Chet Morton. Frank and Joe, starting up, blinked sleepily. "Chet's having a nightmare," thought Joe.

But as he became wider awake, he saw a tall shadowy figure hovering over the bundle that was Chet Morton!

· 17 ·

Help!

As FRANK and Joe got out of their sleeping bags, to spring upon the intruder, Chet Morton unexpectedly began to guffaw.

"Aw, stop it! Ha-ha! Cut it out, will you?"

The black figure had not moved, but Chet was thrashing about on the ground, laughing convulsively.

"Chet!" Joe cried as he groped for his torch. Then he muttered to Frank, "Has he gone out of his mind?"

"N-no," gasped Chet. "Stop licking my face, Mystery! How can a fellow talk?"

Two torch beams illuminated the scene in the same instant. Standing nearby was the mute boy, Simon. The little beagle, with tail whipping about happily, was leaping on Chet with fierce affection.

"Oh, boy!" Joe exclaimed, grinning, "You gave us a scare, Simon."

"We can't keep Mystery with us now," said Frank. "We don't know where we'll be from one day to the next."

Scooping up Mystery with a quick movement, Frank thrust the animal into Simon's arms. "Simon, please look after our dog a little longer. Okay?"

To their astonishment, Simon placed the beagle on the ground. Then, pointing quickly at Frank, Joe, and

Chet in succession, he waved them away frantically with both arms.

"He says for us to clear out," interpreted Joe. "He must mean we're in some danger! What is it, Simon?"

Frank had already put pad and pencil into the mute boy's hands. Now, while Frank and Joe shone their lights on the page, he quickly sketched a picture of a small, windowless cabin, with a gun barrel pointing menacingly from the door!

"Donner's place," Joe muttered. "And he has a gun. Well, we knew that already. We weren't going near there tonight, anyhow."

"Hold on," Frank warned. "He's drawing something else."

Simon had not yet finished. Next to the cabin he drew sketches of two owls seated side by side. With amazing skill, Simon sketched in the fierce owl eyes and beak of each. But one of the birds had high-pointed ear tufts; the other seemed to have no ears at all, and had a round, mask-like face similar to that of a monkey.

"Great sketches," Joe commented. One of his hobbies was ornithology. Now, studying the drawings, he told the others, "The one with the prominent ears is the screech owl. He does the wailing. And monkey face, here, is the barn owl. He does the screeching."

"Hey! What are you doing?" Chet asked suddenly.

Simon, after drawing two very accurate pictures, suddenly took his pencil and crossed them both out. Once again he waved the boys away from him.

"I don't get it," said Frank, puzzled. "Are you afraid of the owls?" Simon shook his head vigorously.

"Do you connect their cries with the witch of Black

Hollow and want to protect us from her?" Again Simon shook his head.

"Maybe he means Donner is going to shoot the owls," suggested Chet. More denials.

"I give up," said Joe. "But listen, Simon. Witches, owls, Donner—nobody is going to drive us out of these woods! We're staying! Get it?"

Peering intently at the determined faces of his new friends, the strange boy looked frustrated. He gathered up Mystery in his arms, and as silently as he had appeared, glided off amongst the trees

"Wish I knew what he was driving at," Chet remarked.

Meanwhile, Frank and Joe had switched off their torches to save the batteries. As the three stood together in silence, a faint flicker appeared in the sky.

"Lightning," Frank commented. "Very far away as yet. Must mean a storm's coming, though. I wish there was a cave, without rattlesnakes, for us to take shelter in."

"Don't worry," Joe assured him. "The storm's far away; it may never reach here. Let's get some shut-eye."

Thoroughly tired, the three friends lay down once more and fell asleep immediately. Some time later Joe suddenly found himself wide awake. His heart was pounding violently. The luminous dial of his watch told him that nearly two hours had passed.

The darkness seemed thicker, the air heavier than a few hours earlier.

"Frank! Chet! Did you hear it?"

"Yes," came Frank's tense, whispered answer. "There it is again!"

The heavy, oppressive silence was shattered by a scream—a horrible drawn-out cry. Again it sounded, this time harsher and higher-pitched. Then a third time.

"That's a human being in touble!" exclaimed Frank, leaping to his feet. "Quick! Roll up your sleeping bags and shove 'em out of sight underneath these bushes. Let's go! Somebody needs our help!"

"This witch may be more real than we thought," said Chet as he hurriedly slipped into his shoes. "Do you suppose she's—she's torturing Captain Maguire?"

Fully awake now, and every sense alert, the boys listened intently while the blood-chilling screams were repeated. To add to the weirdness, the woods were illuminated by a flash of lightning.

"That cry was in the hollow, and not too far from here," Frank directed. "Let's go!"

"Turn on both torches!" Joe called as he rushed forward. "Speed is important!"

The three boys dashed along the path into Black Hollow.

"Halt!" Frank ordered, as the screams came once more. Carefully he placed their direction. "We won't go down to the floor of the valley," he decided. "The cries seem to be coming more from the side. We'll stick to this upper path instead!"

Once again the young detectives rushed forward, halfway up the steep, partly wooded side of the hollow. But within a few seconds Frank halted them again.

"Now what?" Joe asked breathlessly. "I don't hear any more screaming."

"There's something else. Don't you hear it?" Straining his ears to their utmost, Frank listened intently.

But hearing was difficult, for the night was no longer a quiet one. The wind that comes before a thunderstorm was now sweeping through the hollow like an onrushing wave. In the frequent flicker of lightning, huge trees could be seen waving widly and showing the pale undersides of their leaves. Their limbs creaked. The wind hissed in the leaves. But through it all, Frank's ears seemed to detect another sound.

"What is it?" queried Joe.

"A kind of thin, human voice calling. But with this wind, I can't be sure!"

Just then, there came a long flicker of lightning. Joe pointed to a nearby tree. Perched motionless on a branch was a full-grown owl, its huge eyes unblinking even in the vivid glare. Then darkness closed in again.

Suddenly the air was rent by a terrifying scream from the valley floor! Frank, Joe, and Chet were startled. As they crouched, breathless, upon the rock where they had halted, the snap of twigs on the ground alerted them to the movement of a heavy body in the woods just below.

Frank and Joe kept their eyes fixed upon a small grassy clearing to their left.

Suddenly something huge, black, and solid, moving cat-like upon all fours, padded unhurriedly into the grassy area. Then noiselessly it glided into the blackness of the trees on the other side.

"A wildcat!" Joe's heart raced with excitement. "So that's what's been making those horrible screams!"

"But this isn't wildcat country!" Frank protested.

"Hush!" Joe signalled.

Over the sound of the wind and the growl of thunder, the boys distinctly made out a thin, quavering voice.

"Skip-py!" it called. "Skip-py!"

"Good grief, it's Bobby Thompson!" Chet cried out in horror. "He's down there looking for his lost dog!"

"He must be somewhere amongst those trees ahead, where that big cat disappeared just now!" exclaimed Frank.

As he spoke, the howling scream of the mysterious cat-like beast ripped through the night once more. From the same direction came a little boy's frightened sobbing:

"Oh, Skippy, where are you? I want my mother. Help!"

Frantically Frank, Joe, and Chet raced forward, stumbling along the rocky side of the hollow. The big cat sounded off again. Bobby Thompson's pathetic whimpering grew louder and nearer.

"Oh-h, I'm afraid! I want to go home!"

"He must be round here somewhere! Bobby!" Joe called out. "Stay where you are and don't move!"

Suddenly the path of the three boys was blocked by the spreading limbs and branches of a large tree, growing up from the floor of the hollow just below. Bobby's sobs seemed very close now!

In desperation, Frank, Joe, and Chet swept the valley floor below with the beams of their torches. At first they saw only the storm-whipped branches of the trees.

"There!" cried Frank at last.

The yellow beams had finally located the little boy. Wearing a jersey and short trousers, he stood cowering at the base of the big tree just below them. He was hiding his face with one arm, and had raised the other in an effort to protect himself.

A few short yards away, a pair of malevolent green eyes glowed in the torch beams.

Unblinkingly, the eyes stared at their prey. The big animal coughed deep in its throat. The tail lashed about savagely as the beast crouched for the kill.

·18·

A Harrowing Rescue

FRANK Hardy appraised the situation in a single swift glance. With an iron nerve, he issued crisp orders.

"Joe, you're the lightest. Into the tree! You haul Bobby up! Chet, this boulder is loose from the rain. Put your back to it. Roll it down on that cat!"

Meanwhile, Frank shone the beam of his torch directly into the eyes of the cat, in an an effort to delay the creature's death-dealing spring as long as possible.

Joe had already swung himself into the big tree. In another moment he had crawled out on the low-hanging limb directly over Bobby's head. Seeing the beams of the toches, the small boy looked up and spotted Joe. But Joe and the branch were several feet out of Bobby's reach!

Thinking quickly, Joe hooked his knees over one limb, and his toes underneath another. Head downward, reaching with both arms, he swung into space between the cat and the boy

"Bobby! Grab my hands! Quick!"

Paralysed with fear, Bobby hesitated. In the same instant, the powerful black beast with a snarl, shot forward. There was a sudden loud crash of bushes. The animal whirled, then jumped lightly sideways to dodge the heavy boulder tumbling down the hillside.

Quickly Joe grabbed Bobby's thin wrist and yanked the boy, one-handed, upwards until he could grasp Bobby's waist with his other arm. Then with a tremendous effort, he snapped both himself and Bobby into a sitting position of safety upon the limb.

Frustrated, the big cat raged for a moment on the ground below. Then it disappeared in the woods.

Sweating profusely from his effort, Joe handed the limp boy through the branches of the tree to Frank.

"Nice work with that rock, Chet," Joe gasped, as he fought to recover his breath. "It gave me the extra second I needed!"

Bobby Thompson was sobbing again, but now it was with relief, as he buried his face against Frank's chest.

"Don't worry, Bobby, old fellow," said Chet. "We'll take you home. We know where your dog is, and we're going to get him back!"

"Honest?" Bobby asked.

With Chet lighting the way in front, Frank followed carrying the exhausted boy. Joe watched the rear, in case the cat might still be stalking them. The boys worked their way across the side of the hollow until they reached the path.

Soon they had climbed into the clearing, near the ruins of Captain Maguire's cabin. Forked lightning now zigzagged across the sky, showing great piles of menacing clouds. But the rushing wind had already passed over, and between the crashes of thunder came lulls of dead silence.

"Look! What's that?" called Joe, pointing off into the distance. The boys had stopped to rest on the very rim of the hollow.

"You mean those lights way down at the other end of the valley?" asked Chet.

"Yes. If my sense of direction is right," continued Joe with rising excitement, "those lights are on the rim of the hollow just above Walter Donner's place!"

"You're right," agreed Frank. "Something is going on over there, fellows, and I don't think it has anything to do with witches!"

"Let's get Bobby home," urged Chet. "Then we can go over there and see what it's all about."

On the double now, Frank, Joe, and Chet hurried with the little boy to where they had parked the convertible. Soon they were racing down steep Rim Road.

Veering sharply, Frank pulled into the rutted drive by the side of the Thompsons' house. Lights were on in all of the rooms. As the car stopped, Mrs Thompson, nearly hysterical, flew out from the door.

"You must help me! My little boy! He's been gone since supper. I'm so afraid he's lost in the woods, and there's been that terrible scream . . ."

"Hi, Mummy!" said Bobby sleepily from Frank's arms. "Don't worry. I'm okay."

Open-mouthed, the astonished mother stared for a moment. Then snatching her son, she folded him in her arms.

"He was looking for his dog, and I guess he got lost," Chet explained, thinking it wise to say nothing of the mysterious cat-like beast for the time being. "But we're going to bring back his dog, too. Aren't we, Bobby?"

Suddenly Mrs Thompson looked at them intensely. "Tell me," she demanded, "where did you find him? Not in Black Hollow!"

"Yes, we did, Mrs Thompson," Frank answered. "But don't worry, he's okay. I think it would be best if you put him right to bed. We'll be back to explain everything in the morning."

The amazed and grateful woman called her thanks as the three youths jumped into their car. The wheels spun on the gravel, then the car started up the hill.

"Now," Frank told the others, "we'll drive right round the rim. Hang on to your seats, because it isn't much of a road."

Joe and Chet, peering ahead, saw that Frank was right. The road soon narrowed to a pair of wheel ruts, and in places was dangerously close to the edge of the hollow. A single wrong twist of the wheel could mean a fatal plunge into the valley below.

Frank drove swiftly, but with a firm hand. Though bushes and low branches smacked against the windscreen, he did not slow down.

"What's this ahead?" he said suddenly.

The headlights had picked up a vehicle. Joe jumped out to investigate.

"Just an old jalopy, probably abandoned there a year or so ago," he reported as he got back in the car. "It's parked on the very edge of the bank."

Frank drove on towards the mysterious lights they had seen earlier. All at once he stopped the car. They had reached a wider space in the road.

"There's room here to turn around. We might want to get out of those woods in a hurry. I think I'll play it safe."

He turned the convertible back in the direction of Maguire's clearing. "Now, let's go. We can't be more than five minutes from those lights."

There were no sounds except those of the storm, which was just about to break. A flash of lightning and the crack of thunder came simultaneously. It was followed by a continual rumble, and lightning was so frequent that torches were unnecessary. Stealthily Frank, Joe, and Chet crept forward along the narrow track.

Suddenly a man's voice was heard saying, "Here! Grab on to the other end of this, will you!"

Quickly the boys ducked into the cover of some bushes. Ahead of them the lightning showed up the dark bulk of a heavy truck. As they watched, two men, struggling and puffing, lifted a long box from the back of the truck and carried it between them amongst the trees at the edge of the hollow.

"Where are they going with it?" Joe wondered in a whisper. "They'll fall over the edge if they're not careful."

Tense but patient, the youths waited. Still the two men did not reappear.

By now the Hardys were rapidly putting two and two together. The once-baffling clues in the strange case began to fall into place, like the pieces of a jigsaw puzzle.

"Listen!" said Frank. "You know the two owls Simon drew, then crossed out? Now that I think of it, he must have meant the birds don't make the sounds. Their cries are man-made. They're signals to these men with the truck: one to stay away, one to come to the hollow. I wonder which is which?"

"Not only that," Joe added. "Someone is playing witch, using the old story of the missing dogs and screams to scare people away while this unloading is going on."

"I'll bet one of the stolen dogs was parcelled out by Donner to those hijackers we caught in the school van," put in Chet. "The dog acted friendly at first, but the crooks must have trained him to attack on command."

"Sure," Joe declared. "Walter Donner and his gang are hijackers. Probably they're the same gang that Dad is trying to track down."

"Remember how Donner laughed at the police for not catching the thieves?" Frank reminded them. "He thinks he's pretty clever!"

"Captain Maguire probably suspected something," he went on. "He came down to investigate and, I'm afraid, was taken prisoner or something worse."

"But if he's a prisoner"—Joe puzzled—"where are they keeping him? . . . Say, remember the door we heard closing in Donner's kitchen, but didn't see—that may be the answer!"

Eager now to learn more, the three friends grew more impatient by the minute as the two men failed to return to the truck.

"We must trail them." Frank decided. "One at a time, and watch out. We can't afford to get caught in a trap now."

First, Frank slipped cautiously from bush to bush, past the silent truck to the trees at the top of the hollow. Joe followed, then Chet.

Warily they peered ahead. The two hijackers were nowhere to be seen. Frank led his companions through the narrow belt of trees and out on to the exposed edge of the bank. Again they stopped to reconnoitre.

Frank, Joe, and Chet were now crouching in the narrow ridge of small bushes that grew along the rim. Directly in front of them was nothing but bare rocks, curving sharply to the floor of the hollow below.

By now the wind had come up again. Behind them, the trees waved wildly, and even in the bushes the boys could feel its force. Constant flashes of lightning threw a clear white light over everything—so clear that every individual tree in Black Hollow stood out distinctly.

By leaning forward slightly, the boys could see the roof of Walter Donner's cabin and the small clearing surrounding it. There were Donner's sheep, moving nervously in their three-sided pen. But to the boys' amazement, there was absolutely no trace of the hijackers!

"They're not up here and they're not down there," whispered Joe, bewildered. "Anyhow, how could they get down there, especially with that heavy box? These rocks are much too steep!"

Baffled, the boys worked their way along the rim directly above the Donner cabin. Joe led the way, examining the rock face for some possible way into the hollow below.

Suddenly Frank cried out from behind Joe. But the cry was choked off. Turning, Joe and Chet found that their companion had vanished completely, as though swallowed by the earth!

· 19 ·

Prisoners!

"FRANK!" Joe and Chet shouted, throwing aside all caution. "Frank! Where are you?"

The only answer was a white glare of lightning lasting fully three seconds. They could see everything around them plainly. There was no doubt about it: Frank Hardy had disappeared as completely as the two men carrying the box!

"Oh, *where* is he?" Joe cried in despair, his words drowned out by a terrific blast of thunder.

Now, at last, as though split open wide by the latest bolt, the swollen clouds released their load of rainfall in one vast rush. Sheets of water struck the trees with a crash, and hit the rocks with a loud smacking sound.

But in spite of the tumult, a faint human cry from the ground underneath them reached Joe's keen ears.

"Over here!" he shouted, groping through the downpour to a wide, round bush from which the cry seemed to have come.

"Help!" Joe cried suddenly.

The ground gave way beneath his feet. For an instant he felt himself falling in space. But in that moment the strong arms of Chet Morton hooked under his armpits and hauled him back to safety.

Snapping on their torches, the two boys trained the light downwards and discovered the mouth of a deep, wide hole, cleverly hidden by the round bush. As they peered below in amazement at a narrow wooden slide, a familiar voice, sounding far away, called up from below.

"Joe! Chet!" It was Frank.

Carefully Joe and Chet sat down on the slide, grasping the sides. In spite of their caution, they were soon whizzing through the darkness. They tumbled in a heap at the bottom but quickly leaped to their feet.

"Turn on your torches," directed Frank. "I lost mine when I fell."

The yellow beam suddenly lit up a fairly high, rock-walled chamber, with passages leading from it in several directions.

"Must be the gang's hide-out," said Joe in a low voice. "And they slide their stolen goods down that chute."

Cautiously the three friends moved along one of the rock passageways. Abruptly, it was blocked by a low, wooden door.

"Should we open it?" Joe whispered. "It might be a trap!"

"Can't stop now," muttered Frank. Boldly he stepped forward and pushed. The heavy old door swung noise-lessly inward.

The next instant the Hardys and Chet gasped in disbelief. A single paraffin lamp dimly illuminated the square, rock-hewn room. A man, with a dirty bandage round his dishevelled grey hair, lay upon a camp bed. Slowly he turned dull, sunken eyes upon them.

"Captain Maguire!" cried Frank, rushing forward.

The expression in the man's eyes changed instantly to one of lively hope.

"Frank! Joe! Your father got my letter! Thank goodness. Where is Fenton?" Shakily, the man sat up. Evidently he was still weak from the wound in his head.

"Dad couldn't get here," Frank explained, "so he sent us." Frank introduced Chet, then went on, "We've been hunting you for days, Captain. Right now we must be careful. We don't know where Donner and his gang may be, and we don't want to be captured."

When he heard that the boys were alone, Captain Maguire's joy became mixed with concern. "I can tell you where Donner is," he answered. "He and several of his pals are in the cabin. There's a passageway to it through the other door." He pointed to one across the room.

As the captain paused, the boys noticed his torn shirt—the scraps they had found in the hollow were of the same material.

"You must go for help, boys," he urged. "This gang has been hijacking equipment intended for the nose cones of rockets. They've also been stealing furs, surgical equipment, and whatever else they dare. They're smart, and they'll stop at nothing."

"We'll go back up the shaft," proposed Chet. "I noticed some steps on one side. And we'll take you with us, captain. We couldn't leave you here!"

"But if the gang finds the captain gone now," Frank pointed out thoughtfully, "they'll know the game is up and clear out."

"Frank's right," agreed Maguire.

"You go then, Chet," Joe decided. "Frank and I will stay here and look after the captain."

After Chet had left, Captain Maguire began his story. "When the screams first started, I didn't think much of it. But dogs began disappearing, too. So, recalling the hex legend, I began noting on my calendar the dates on which I heard the screams, as well as any dogs that were missing. Soon I became convinced there was a connection, and that something underhand was going on. I even suspected the hollow might be a hide-out for the hijackers. That's why I sent for your father. Then one night my cocker spaniel Ginger was stolen and I decided to investigate alone."

The boys nodded and Frank said, "And that's when you were captured."

"Yes," the captain replied sadly. "I took my gun that night and began searching the hollow. I heard something in the bushes and asked who it was. There was no answer. Then I saw two glaring eyes and heard a scream. It was a puma. I gave it both barrels, but missed."

"Yes, we found your shells," said Joe.

"Donner heard the shots, sneaked up behind, and slugged me," the captain continued. "The next thing I knew I was in his cabin, and he was pushing aside a section of the rock wall in the kitchen. There was a wooden door behind it.

"I pretended I was still out. He dragged me down a passageway, past a room with a barred door, then under the low door to this room, and dumped me on this bed. I've been here ever since. My only hope has been that your father had received my letter and would try to find me."

"And all the time Dad was working on the same case over in New Jersey!" Joe marvelled.

Quickly Frank informed the captain of the boys' own sleuthing, including Webber's claim that Maguire owed him money.

*Frank and Joe were prodded by Donner's gun down
the rock passageway*

"A lie," said the captain in disgust. "Just an excuse to spy on you boys at the cabin."

Frank concluded his account with the boys' suspicion that the owl sounds were being made by humans and used as signals.

"You're right there," confirmed Maguire. "I've learned that much since I've been here. Donner warns the hijackers not to come by faking the *screech* of the *barn* owl. I guess he's been using it a lot since you got here!"

"Then, the *wailing* of the *screech* owl means the coast is clear. It's okay to deliver the goods," Joe finished.

"That's absolutely right!" came a deep, familiar voice from the door leading to the cabin.

Whirling, the Hardys found themselves facing the long, silver barrel of Walter Donner's pistol. The gang leader had quietly pushed open the door to the cell and heard the last part of the conversation. He was followed by a big, rough-looking man and the lawyer, Wyckoff Webber.

"My congratulations," said Donner in a mocking tone. "You've solved the case very cleverly through the clue of the screeching owl. By the way, I did the screeching and wailing myself. Pretty good, eh?"

Then the big man's voice took on a tone of menace. "But it won't do you any good. Your reward will be to meet the screaming witch herself!"

Wondering, Frank and Joe were prodded by the muzzle of Donner's gun down the rock passageway towards the cabin and into the cell with the barred door that Captain Maguire had mentioned.

"Socky!" called Donner harshly to the rough-looking man. "Go get that third kid!"

Meanwhile, Frank and Joe looked round the rock-walled room by the feeble light of Donner's torch. They noticed that the rear wall was covered by a tarpaulin. The air was heavy and moist, as in most underground chambers, but there was also a strange rank odour.

"Like your new quarters?" taunted Donner, indicating the rock walls. "All these chambers and passages were hewn out of natural caverns by the Abolitionists when they built the cabin against the front of the rock.

"Very clever people," he went on affably. "They were the ones who revived the witch legend by stealing dogs and faking screams to keep people away from the hollow while they hid runaway slaves. Don't you admire my extensive historical research?"

"At least they had a good motive," said Frank defiantly. "They didn't steal dogs to cover up a hijacking racket. By the way, we know where Bobby Thompson's Skippy is."

Donner looked startled for a moment, then said, "I don't know what you're talking about." He went on mockingly, "I fooled you boys with the hideous face in the woods. It wasn't Simon. I wore a rubber mask and a black wig."

"Skip the talk!" snapped Joe. "What are you going to do with us?"

Realizing that he could not shake the boys' nerve, the tall man abruptly crossed the room to the tarpaulin-covered wall.

"Meet the witch!" cried Donner, ripping away the canvas. The faint light showed the bars of a cage, and behind them, the fierce green eyes and powerful body of a big, tawny-brown puma!

"Some of the screams were his," said Donner. "When I heard that my bother William—Colonel

Thunder—was going to have this beast destroyed because it almost killed him, I sent Socky to get the animal from him. I felt that such a 'pet' would be helpful in reviving the witch legend. But William wasn't told *I* wanted it, nor why.

"The puma knows who's master *here*, at any rate," the gang leader added in a cruel voice. "William and I don't have anything to do with each other, but he did warn my lawyer that some snoopers said I was stealing dogs."

"And then Webber set Captain Maguire's cabin on fire and tried to burn us to death," said Joe, looking sharply at the lawyer's ragged left shoe. But the youth did not reveal his clue as to the tell-tale prints found near the scene of the burnt-out cabin. He was sure Sheriff Ecker's casts of the footprints would be conclusive evidence.

"I deny that!" cried Webber. "You can't prove it!"

"Oh, yes, we can," Joe told him.

Frank interrupted. "This puma was loose in the hollow tonight, wasn't it?"

"That's right," Donner admitted. "I sometimes let him out through the door you see at the rear of his cage. It leads out on to the rocks. But I only let him out after I've put a sleeping pill in his food. He usually comes back quietly.

"However," he added meaningfully, "tonight the effects of his last pill wore off sooner than I expected. That's why I had to warn my men to lie low right after I'd given them the all clear. Fortunately, my pet came back without harming anyone.

"By the way, the grating between yourselves and this animal can be raised—just yank the chain here.

At the same time, the puma's outside door will be raised. So if you want to escape, the way out is very simple. All you have to do is get past the puma!"

Walter Donner stepped back into the passage, slammed the door to the boys' prison, and shot the heavy bolt into place.

"Oh, I forgot to tell you," came his mocking voice from the corridor, "there is another chain, with which I can raise *only* the grating between you and the puma. I'll get round to it sometime tonight."

Luckily, Joe had hidden his torch inside his shirt. Now, left alone, the brothers carefully examined the walls of their prison.

"No way out," concluded Joe. "Our only hope is that Chet got away all right and can return with the police before Donner lifts that grating!"

Switching off the torch, the two boys waited tensely in the pitch darkness. A few feet away the big cat could be heard pacing nervously. After a long silence, Frank and Joe heard voices in the corridor outside.

"Did you get that fat kid?" asked Donner.

"You can forget him, boss," came the rough voice of the strong-arm man, Socky. "I see him pull out in this yellow convertible. So I take off after him in the truck. Pretty soon I see his lights, pretty far ahead, goin' round a turn. Then in a couple of minutes I hear this terrific crash—like a car goin' right over the edge and down in the hollow. I come up, and there's the wreck way down below—burning up like mad. Nobody could've lived through it."

"Good!" snapped Walter Donner. "That takes care of *him!*"

Frank and Joe stood as if frozen, in utter horror!

Triumphant Sleuths

For one long moment the Hardy brothers were too stunned to speak.

"Not Chet! It can't be true!" Joe faltered at last.

"We mustn't believe the story," Frank told him, his voice trembling. "We must get out of here and learn the truth!"

Together the two boys moved up to the grating to study the only possible escape route: past the dangerous puma and out the far door. The beast gave a menacing growl as it stalked to the bars.

"Let's take off our socks, shirts, belts, and sweaters," Frank commanded. "I have a plan."

In a moment the two boys were squatting, stripped to the waist, before a heap of clothing.

"There's one thing every animal respects," muttered Frank. The youth doubled the heavy belts together for a stiff core, and began wrapping the sweaters and shirts around them.

"Fire!" Joe exclaimed, catching on. "You're making a torch! But what about matches?"

After Donner's lecture about preparedness, I vowed I'd never be without them" Frank returned, drawing a watertight cylinder from his pocket.

A match flared in the dark, square room. The puma

growled apprehensively. Slowly the flame crawled up the impromptu torch, growing brighter and brighter until it was a ball of fire.

Panicky now, the big cat loped back and forth, snarling viciously.

"Now, while it lasts!" cried Frank. "Yank that chain, Joe!"

With a scraping sound the iron bars creaked upwards. Holding the flaming torch before him, Frank advanced upon the puma. Plunging, snarling with fear, raising its powerful paws, the beast backed through the outer door, which Joe had opened.

"It's working!" Frank cried as he too stepped outside.

But at that very instant Joe was seized by powerful arms from behind. The snarls of the puma and the sound of the chain had warned the hijackers.

"Socky!" shouted Donner. "Get that other one!"

"Keep going, Frank!" Joe shouted.

One backward glance told Frank what was happening: Joe was going down under two attackers, another one coming for him. Desperately Frank rushed forward and hurled the ball of flame straight into the puma's snarling face. Maddened, the big cat turned tail and plunged for the freedom of the woods. Frank by now was sprinting at top speed in another direction. Socky emerged, hesitated, and started off in pursuit.

Meanwhile, Joe was slowly regaining consciousness after being dealt a stunning blow. His head throbbed. His wrists and ankles stung where ropes cut into the flesh. He was on the damp floor bound hand and foot.

"Now, what kind of 'accident' can we arrange for these two?" It was Donner speaking.

Opening his eyes, Joe saw that he had been moved to Captain Maguire's cell. The captain, also bound lay above him on the bed. A hijacker stood over the two with a pistol, while Walter Donner, holding a lamp aloft in one hand, coolly plotted their murder.

"Perhaps a nice, hot fire that won't leave any evidence," the gang leader suggested. "And we mustn't forget to include your brother—if Socky gets to him before the puma does."

"Hands up!" came a sudden, sharp command. "Drop that gun!"

Spinning round, Donner found himself covered by a gun. Two policemen stood in the doorway where he and Webber had surprised the Hardys earlier!

As Donner's pistol clattered to the floor, he swung his lamp viciously at the nearest officer. There was a crash, and total darkness for a moment. In the confusion, the wily gang leader slipped down the passage to the puma's cage and dashed to freedom.

Frank, meanwhile, had kept sprinting through the woods. He weaved in and out, seeking always to keep some trees between himself and his pursuer. Now and then a pistol cracked behind him. A heavy bullet thumped into a tree, or ripped the leaves above his head.

Completely drenched from his flight through the wet bushes, Frank reached the rocky side of the hollow and clambered upwards. A bullet exploded in the rock beside him, sending painful splinters into his hand.

Realizing that he was too exposed on the open slope, in the pale light of early dawn, Frank ducked behind a big rock and waited.

As the burly Socky toiled upwards in the grey light, Frank lunged towards him in a tremendous tackle. The heavily built man went down with a crash, still clutching his revolver in one hand. Desperately Frank grabbed the man's wrist, knowing that control of the gun meant life or death.

Locked together, the two struggling bodies rolled down the steep slope, bouncing from one level to another. Finally Socky rolled on top, and raised his weapon. But at this moment a figure hurtled out of nowhere, knocking the hijacker's head against a stone and wresting the pistol from him all in one movement.

"Simon!" cried Frank joyously. "How'd you—?"

But the mute boy only indicated by pointing upward that Frank should continue climbing.

"You're right, Simon. I must get help!"

Once more, Frank clambered towards the road at the top. By now it was very light, though the sun had not risen. Frank, looking round, suddenly spotted a man not fifty yards above him going in the same direction. Walter Donner!

The gang leader turned. For a moment he and the young detective stared at each other. Frank set himself for another struggle. But, to his astonishment, Donner turned and began climbing upwards again as fast as he could.

Calling on his muscles for one last all-out effort, Frank scrambled upwards in pursuit.

In another minute Frank hauled himself on to a ledge. Now Donner's legs dangled just above him. Thinking of Chet, lying entangled in the wrecked car, Frank pulled the man down savagely. But a snarl from the ledge just above him, and a sudden terrified scream from Donner, checked his poised fist.

Instinctively Frank pressed both himself and his antagonist against the rock wall, as the two-hundred-pound body of the furious puma hurtled past within inches of their heads. Landing off balance, the beast skidded and tumbled rapidly downhill.

Donner jerked loose. But Frank quickly sent a swift punch to the man's mid-section, following it up with a smashing blow to the jaw. "That's for Chet!" he panted as Donner slumped, unconscious.

"Hi! Up there!" came shouts from below.

Looking down, Frank saw the rocky slope swarming with police. Three of them were throwing a net over the spitting, scrambling puma. Several others had almost reached Frank himself.

"Nice work, boy!" cried the first man to come up. "Donner nearly got away!"

Brushing aside congratulations, Frank asked urgently, "Is my brother Joe all right? Have you examined the car wreck?"

The friendly policeman looked puzzled. "Joe Hardy? Sure, he's okay. But I don't know what wreck you're talking about."

Quickly Frank scrambled back down to the valley floor. "I'll get Joe and we'll—we'll look for Chet," he thought, while jogging swiftly amongst the trees to Donner's cabin.

The door of the stone cabin was wide open. Frank dashed in, then stopped short in utter astonishment.

An appetizing aroma, the sizzle of bacon frying in a pan, the sound of happy voices all talking at once reached him from the kitchen. Frank opened his mouth and stood in speechless wonder.

Joe and Captain Maguire were standing by the secret door, laughing. Seated at the kitchen table were Simon and Fenton Hardy. And presiding over the stove, flipping pancakes vigorously into the air and talking loudly the whole time, was Chet Morton!

"Frank!" his father cried out. "So good to see you! I'm certainly glad this case is solved."

"You knew?"

"One of the policemen sent a short-wave message you were safe and Donner captured."

"But Chet . . . What . . . ? How . . . ?" Frank stammered.

"Nothing to be amazed about," said Chet as the others, grinning, made a place for Frank at the table. "Old Chet went for the police and brought 'em back, that's all!"

"But the smashed car—you weren't in it?"

"Right! Just a little detective's trick." The stout boy shrugged with attempted modesty. "I had a head start on that hijacker, so I hid the convertible in some trees near that jalopy we saw. I put in a blanket, set the old crate on fire, and shoved it over the edge."

Chet beamed. "Did it burn! That Socky thought I was in it. I waited till he'd gone, drove on down Rim Road without lights, and called the police from the first house with a phone. Told 'em to come ready for a wild animal as well as criminals. When they got here I showed the police the secret chute and the cabin. They did the rest, and rounded up all the crooks."

"You're a real trooper for sure," Frank said. "We couldn't solve a mystery without you."

This proved to be true in the boys' next case, *While The Clock Ticked*.

"As for me," Fenton Hardy took up the story, "I hurried over here from New Jersey right after I quizzed that pair you boys caught in the school van. Just by luck, I was at the State Police headquarters when Chet's call came in."

"This *is* the gang you've been after, then?" Frank asked.

"Sure is," his father answered, "and they're all behind bars now. Webber's shoes matched the cast taken by Sheriff Ecker—so he confessed to setting the cabin on fire, hiding nearby, and seeing you boys escape. We found the cache of hijacked goods in two of the underground passages.

"Webber has also confessed to selling everything but the missile nose cones as property of fictitious companies which were going out of business. A clever racket he worked with an auctioneer in New York City."

Joe added, "And he was holding up the settlement of the Donner estate until he and Walter had disposed of all the hijacked goods. The gang confessed they did take that hound dog, and kept it for their own use. Socky was the one who spied on us in the woods, and also on Webber. Donner didn't even trust his own men. By the way, William and his sister are innocent of any part in the racket."

"Well, my job's over now," concluded Mr Hardy. "And you three boys did the major part of it for me. Which means you get the major share of the credit, and the major share of the reward money, too!"

"And they certainly deserve it!" Captain Maguire put in fervently.

"My share's going to Simon," Frank declared immediately. "Dad, perhaps his voice could be restored through surgery!" Joe and Chet instantly seconded Frank's decision.

"I'm sure medical science can do something," Fenton Hardy answered. "Some very successful mechanical speaking devices have been developed, if it should turn out his voice can't be restored in any other way. In any case, we can send him to art school. I understand he has a fine talent for drawing."

"That's for sure," said Chet with admiration, as Simon's eyes shone with gratitude. "I'll have all the reward I want out of this case if I can keep Mystery. But say, I want to make sure Miss Donner gives back Skippy to little Bobby Thompson!"

"It'll be done, Chet," Mr Hardy promised.

"That leaves just the puma," said Joe. "We'll give him to a zoo. They can put up a sign over its cage:

'This Animal Was Once Known and Feared As the Screaming Witch of Black Hollow'

"How about adding a couple of owls?" Chet suggested. "Boy, that screeching really gave me the creeps!"